PARADISE FOUND

Putting his arm roughly around Salrina's neck, the Frenchman dragged her, in the passing of a second, close against him with his back against the wall.

Then he drew a long, thin dagger from his coat and held it against her breast.

For a moment there was a silence of utter astonishment in the gilded room.

Then he said in French:

"One move and this woman dies!"

A Camfield Novel of Love
by Barbara Cartland

". . . she has truly become The Queen of Romance."
—VOGUE

"Barbara Cartland's novels are all distinguished by their intelligence, good sense, and good nature . . ."
—ROMANTIC TIMES

"She is wise and witty . . ."
—NEW YORK DAILY NEWS

Camfield Place,
Hatfield
Hertfordshire,
England

Dearest Reader,

Camfield Novels of Love mark a very exciting era of my books with Jove. They have already published nearly two hundred of my titles since they became my first publisher in America, and now all my original paperback romances in the future will be published exclusively by them.

As you already know, Camfield Place in Hertfordshire is my home, which originally existed in 1275, but was rebuilt in 1867 by the grandfather of Beatrix Potter.

It was here in this lovely house, with the best view in the county, that she wrote *The Tale of Peter Rabbit*. Mr. McGregor's garden is exactly as she described it. The door in the wall that the fat little rabbit could not squeeze underneath and the goldfish pool where the white cat sat twitching its tail are still there.

I had Camfield Place blessed when I came here in 1950 and was so happy with my husband until he died, and now with my children and grandchildren, that I know the atmosphere is filled with love and we have all been very lucky.

It is easy here to write of love and I know you will enjoy the Camfield Novels of Love. Their plots are definitely exciting and the covers very romantic. They come to you, like all my books, with love.

Bless you,

CAMFIELD NOVELS OF LOVE
by Barbara Cartland

Other books by Barbara Cartland

A NEW CAMFIELD NOVEL OF LOVE BY

BARBARA CARTLAND

Paradise Found

A JOVE BOOK

PARADISE FOUND

A Jove Book / published by arrangement with
the author

PRINTING HISTORY
Jove edition / September 1985

ISBN: 0-515-08340-2

Jove books are published by The Berkley Publishing Group,
200 Madison Avenue, New York, N.Y. 10016.
The words "A JOVE BOOK" and the "J" with sunburst
are trademarks belonging to Jove Publications, Inc.

PRINTED IN THE UNITED STATES OF AMERICA

Author's Note

THE Prince Regent liked young Bucks and Beaux around him, but as he grew older his parties at Carlton House began to bore him.

The long drawn-out dinners with a great number of *entrées* from the Regent's French chefs did not compensate for the lack of stimulating conversation that had been so much a part of the years when Mrs. Fitzherbert was the hostess.

The Marchioness of Hertford and, later, the Marchioness of Coyningham were inclined to monopolise the guests' attention to their own advantage.

However, Carlton House was a brilliant contrast compared to the gloom and darkness that surrounded Buckingham Palace, and no matter how old and fat the Regent became, he was still very witty and had an eye for a beautiful picture and a beautiful woman.

Paradise Found

chapter one

1814

THE Earl of Fleetwood tied his cravat before the mirror over the fireplace with a dexterity that always infuriated his valet.

But he preferred to be self-sufficient and had often said there was no work carried out in his various houses that he could not do better than those he paid to do it.

Watching him from the bed, Lady Oline Blunham thought that no man could be more attractive.

Her eyes roved over the Earl's square shoulders, under his thin lawn shirt, his slender waist and narrow hips tapering down to long legs that every bootmaker extolled as being the perfect shape for the fashionable Hessians.

The Earl's lovemaking had been fiery, passionate, and extremely satisfying.

But strangely enough, he was not thinking of the beauty

of Lady Oline as she lay back against her lace-edged pillows, but of a small object that he had placed on the marble mantelpiece in front of him.

He had actually stepped on it when he got out of bed, and as it had hurt the sole of his foot, he had picked it up, looked at it curiously, then set it down as he started to dress.

Now, as his cravat was finished to his satisfaction and encircled his neck tightly, keeping the points of his collar high above his chin in the fashion decreed by Beau Brummell, the Earl said:

"Has your husband changed his shirtmakers lately?"

Oline Blunham gave a little giggle.

"What a funny question! No, of course not! Edward has been to Jackson in Jermyn Street ever since he left Eton and would no more think of patronising any other shirtmaker than of leaving Westons, who make his coats!"

"I thought that was so," the Earl said, "and I too find Jackson the best shirtmaker in London."

He touched for a moment the button at the bottom of his shirt as if to make certain that it did not resemble the one at which he was looking.

Then he picked up his close-fitting coat, shrugged himself into it, and pulled the revers into shape.

It would have been impossible, he thought as he turned round, for any Gentleman of Fashion to be more elegant, and at the same time more masculine.

With a little cry Oline Blunham held out her arms.

"If you must go, Alaric," she said softly, "kiss me good-bye before you do so."

The Earl looked at her for a long moment.

She was certainly very lovely with her dark hair falling over her white shoulders and her eyes which had a touch of green in them pleading with him, while her red lips were provocatively inviting.

But there was actually a hard expression on his face and a tightness to the line of his lips before he said:

"Thank you, Oline, for the pleasure you have given me, but it appears that your last visitor left something behind, which he might miss."

As he spoke the Earl walked to the bed, put the shirt button he had taken from the mantelpiece into Lady Blunham's hand, and closed her fingers over it.

"What are you ... saying? What are you ... talking about?" she asked in an agitated manner.

There was no answer because the Earl had already gone and all she could hear were his footsteps going quietly down the stairs.

She opened her hand, saw what lay on her soft pink palm, and with a scream of fury threw it across the room.

The Earl closed the door of Blunham House in Queen Street, and walking swiftly in the dim light of the dawn, reached his own house in Berkeley Square a few minutes later.

A tired night footman managed to stifle his yawns as he let His Lordship in.

Then locking the door he went back to the comfortable padded chair in which he intended to sleep until awakened by the housemaids coming down soon after five o'clock to start cleaning and dusting.

The Earl, however, was not yawning as he walked up the curving staircase and along the passage to his bedroom.

He was, in fact, thinking that if there was one thing that annoyed him, it was a mistress being unfaithful to him.

That they were unfaithful to their husbands was taken for granted by the fashionable Society in which he moved.

But what he would not accept was a woman who professed her love for him keeping her bed warm with other lovers in his absence.

It had not struck him during the three days he had been away in the country that Oline would, despite her protestations of undying love, take another lover.

He thought now he might have guessed she was insatiable and what it really came down to was that for her one man was very like another.

He was, however, conceited enough to think he was very special to the women on whom he bestowed his favours, and while Edward Blunham might be prepared to "turn a blind eye" to his wife's infidelity, it was something he had no intention of doing.

The Earl was fastidious and had certain rules thought up by himself to which he rigidly conformed.

Although it was fashionable for anybody in his position to pursue the much-acclaimed Beauties of the *Beau Monde*, it was also considered correct for any Gentleman who could afford it—and it was an expensive pastime— to keep a pretty "Cyprian" at the same time.

This was against the Earl's private code, and he conducted no more than one love affair at a time and with an ardour and expertise that had gained him the reputation of being irresistible.

While he more or less dedicated himself to the woman in whom he was interested, he expected the same response from her.

He knew as he got into the large comfortable bed in which a number of his ancestors had been born and died that he would not call on Oline Blunham again.

4

He then erased her from his mind as if, in fact, she had never existed.

* * *

Later in the morning the Earl, despite a somewhat strenuous night, had ridden in the Park on a horse he had recently bought at Tattersall's and which had required all his considerable expertise to control.

He was enjoying a late breakfast in the Dining Room when the door opened and his friend Lord Charles Egham came in.

"Good morning, Charles," the Earl said without looking up from *The Morning Post*, which he was reading while eating.

"You are late!" Charles Egham replied. "I am not surprised, remembering that I saw you leave the ball with Oline."

The Earl did not reply, which did not surprise his friend, who knew only too well that he never talked about his love affairs.

Lord Charles therefore helped himself to a dish of sweetbreads cooked with fresh mushrooms brought from the country very early that morning.

Then sitting down at the table he began to eat with relish.

"What are you going to do today?" he asked when his immediate hunger was somewhat satisfied.

"I am going to the country," the Earl replied.

His friend stared at him in astonishment.

"You are going to the country? But you only returned yesterday!"

"Yes, I know, but there is nothing to keep me in

London, and I have two horses I want to break in. Come and help me!"

Lord Charles was still staring at him.

"I cannot understand you, Alaric," he said. "When you got back yesterday there were a dozen invitations waiting for you, and I heard you tell your secretary to accept them all."

"I have changed my mind."

There was a little pause, then Lord Charles said knowingly:

"Oline being difficult?"

"I know nobody of that name!" the Earl replied abruptly.

Lord Charles sat back in his chair with a twinkle in his eye as he said:

"I think I can guess the reason for this change of heart."

"You can keep your guessing to yourself!" the Earl said sharply. "I have no wish to discuss it. Are you, or are you not, coming with me to the country?"

"Of course I am!" Lord Charles replied. "I have not had a decent meal since you went away, and I always think your Chef at Fleet is even better than your man here."

He rose as he spoke to help himself to another dish from the sideboard.

There was over a half dozen of them, and Lord Charles hesitated between two, then compromised by taking a little of both.

The Earl did not attend to him. He knew only too well that as the younger son of an impoverished Duke, Charles found it not only hard to get enough to eat, but there was certainly no chance of his riding a decent horse, if he could not rely on him.

He and Charles Egham had been at Eton together, and they had also served for three years in the same Regiment, although Alaric on the death of his father had been obliged to buy himself out.

The Earl had, as it happened, been reading a report on Wellington's Army, which having fought its way through Spain, was now threatening Napoleon in the South of France.

He laid down *The Morning Post* and said:

"I have a damned good mind, Charles, to join up again, whatever Prinny may say about it."

"You have suggested it before," Lord Charles replied, "but His Royal Highness made it quite clear that he has no wish for anybody so distinguished as yourself to be either killed or taken prisoner."

"I know he said that," the Earl said crossly, "but this is a free country, and if I want to fight for it, I shall do so!"

"I understand your feelings, at the same time you know as well as I do that there is a great deal to be done on your estates, and if you are not there I doubt if the new land you have brought under cultivation to provide the country's need will be so successful."

The Earl pushed his plate away from in front of him and put his arms on the table before he said:

"I find it extremely frustrating to sit here in England going from Ball to Ball and from woman to woman when I should be helping to put an end to Napoleon's tyranny over the rest of Europe."

"If you feel so strongly about it, I should have another word with the Regent!"

The Earl pushed aside his cup of coffee.

"I know exactly what he will say," he replied, "and I have the uncomfortable feeling that Wellington will say the same thing. I cannot think why my father had to die before the war was over!"

"By all accounts it will not be long now," Lord Charles said cheerfully. "They say Napoleon is getting desperate, and there is no doubt that Wellington is moving into France more quickly than anybody had expected."

The Earl sighed and sat back in his chair petulantly.

"I want to be with him!"

"What has upset you?" Charles asked sympathetically.

"I do not think it is any one particular thing," the Earl replied. "It is just the incredible boredom of knowing what will happen day after day, night after night."

He paused before he added fiercely:

"I want action! I want excitement! I want what we had when we were together in Portugal."

"Discomfort and fleas!"

Despite himself the Earl laughed.

"That is certainly true. I shall never forget the filth of the houses in which we had to sleep and of the women who were always hanging about the Camp."

"If you want the truth," Lord Charles said, "I think we are both a bit too old for that now, and if you do not appreciate a soft bed, with or without a companion in it, I do!"

The Earl laughed again, then he said:

"You always cheer me up, Charles. Let us go to the country. I find my horses a good deal more interesting and certainly more unexpected than the women with whom we spend our time!"

Lord Charles gave the Earl a quick glance out of the

corner of his eye, and thought that Oline Blunham had certainly overplayed her hand last night.

He was used to the Earl becoming quickly bored with any woman who took his fancy, but he had known when he saw him before dinner that he was looking forward to being with Oline again.

He had been quite certain that, unless something had changed her considerably, she was waiting for him with a palpitating heart.

All women had palpitating hearts where the Earl was concerned, and while inevitably he was the one who tired first, it was not usual for there to be such a dramatic turnabout as seemed to be happening at the moment.

He was however too tactful to say this out loud, and instead as he spread a piece of toast thickly with Jersey butter from the Earl's Home Farm, he said:

"I had better go and pack my things. I presume you will be driving your Phaeton?"

"Of course," the Earl said. "But there is no need for you to trouble yourself. Send a footman to tell your man to pack everything you require and to bring it round immediately in a Hackney carriage."

He rang the gold bell that stood on the table beside him as he spoke, and as he did so the door was opened immediately by the Butler and Lord Charles gave his order.

"You can tell Danvers I shall be leaving in an hour," the Earl added.

"You'll be going to Fleet, M'Lord?"

"Yes."

"Very good, M'Lord. I'll see that everything is ready."

The Butler shut the door and Lord Charles laughed.

"I always wonder," he said, "if the day will come when Danvers looks astonished at one of your commands or actually queries it."

"Why should he?" the Earl asked.

"Because you are unpredictable, my dear Alaric, and at times you even leave me gasping."

"You are talking nonsense!" the Earl said, rising as he spoke. "There is nothing unpredictable about preferring the country to London and the inane conversation that takes place at every party when inevitably one knows beforehand what everybody is going to say."

He walked out of the Dining Room as he spoke and Lord Charles knew he was going to the Library.

There his letters would have already been opened for him by his Secretary and those that required a reply put in a neat pile awaiting his verdict.

Lord Charles took a quick sip from his cup of coffee and taking a large apple out of the Sèvres bowl in the centre of the table started to peel it as he followed the Earl.

When they reached the Library, a pleasant room lined with books and overlooking the small courtyard at the back of the house, the Earl threw open the window as if he needed air.

Lord Charles having eaten half the apple threw the rest of it into one of the flower beds.

"If you were not in such a hurry to go to the country," he said as the Earl did not speak, "I was going to suggest that you might meet an extremely attractive 'Bit o' Muslin' who has during the last two days become the toast of St. James's."

"I am not interested!" the Earl said firmly. "What I want, Charles, is adventure, some sort of excitement that does not smell of an exotic scent and can talk of nothing but love!"

"What else is there to talk about?"

"If only I had something to throw at you!" the Earl said, sitting down at the desk. "As it is, I know you are only trying to provoke me and since you will go on nagging like any shrewish wife until I tell you what you want to know, I have finished with Oline!"

"I guessed that," Lord Charles said. "I suppose you found out about Napier!"

"So that is who it was!" the Earl exclaimed.

"They have been very careful in case you got wind of it," Lord Charles went on. "I happened to see them only by chance going into a private room at the White House."

The White House was the most fashionable "Palace of Pleasure" in the West End.

As the Earl well knew, there were private rooms on the first floor where two people who did not wish to be seen could dine very discreetly and enter and leave by a side door.

"What were you doing at the White House?" he asked. "You know as well as I do you cannot afford their ridiculously exorbitant charges."

"That is something I have no intention of telling you," Lord Charles replied.

"In other words, she paid!"

Then he laughed.

"I can see you being led into trouble, Charlie, and the sooner you come to the country with me the better!"

"Which means you are running away! But I am still interested as to how you learnt about Napier."

"He left his 'visiting card' behind in the shape of a

shirt button!" the Earl said briefly.

Lord Charles threw himself back in his chair and went into peals of laughter.

"A shirt button!" he cried. "Only you, Alaric, would notice anything so insignificant and unimportant."

"As a matter of fact, I stood on it barefooted!" the Earl remarked.

Lord Charles laughed until the tears came into his eyes. Then he said:

"You are quite right, all this is beneath your dignity and your importance. There must be something better for us to do."

"If there is, let us go and find it," the Earl replied.

Lord Charles had brought the expression of good temper back to his handsome face, and his lips were no longer set in a hard line.

It was difficult when they were together not to behave as they always had, and when they first joined the Army they had been known to the officers and the men alike as "The Terrible Twins."

They always seemed to be in trouble of some sort, and yet they were envied because they appeared to enjoy life more than anybody else.

In spite of the rioting and drinking they had indulged in when they first left School, everybody who knew them had to admit that they were both highly intelligent and well informed on many subjects about which their contemporaries knew very little.

But whatever escapades they thought up when they were in the Army, the men under them were better looked after, smarter, and a great deal happier than any other troops in the whole of Portugal.

The Earl had lately been offered a Ministerial Post in

the Foreign Office, if he wished to take it.

But while he felt honoured by such a suggestion, he could not help feeling that to be confined to a desk in the Ministry would make him feel frustrated.

He therefore thanked the Prime Minister, who had offered him the position, and made the excuse that he still had a great deal of work to do on his various estates.

As the Prime Minister knew the Earl was contributing a great deal to the war effort by increasing the production of food that was so vitally needed, he had not pressed him further.

The Prince Regent however had very different ideas. He enjoyed the Earl's company as he enjoyed Lord Charles's, and insisted on both of them being in attendance on him whenever possible.

It was the Earl who rebelled first.

"If I have to eat one more dinner of over twelve *entrées,*" he said, "I shall go on a hunger strike!"

"It is not so much the food that I object to," Lord Charles confided, "it is the heat of the rooms at Carlton House. God knows why 'Prinny' will never open a window!"

"He feels the cold."

"But he is so fat! His superfluous flesh should protect him from chills of every sort!"

There was no need to say any more and they both began to make excuses when the Regent commanded their presence.

It was difficult to be evasive for long, and only by going to the country could the Earl escape the long drawn-out meals and musical evenings, or, worse still, the Fetes that the Regent insisted on giving at Carlton House whenever he could think up an excuse for one.

The only consolation, Charles found, was that despite the Regent's preoccupation with older women, every beauty in London sooner or later found her way into the Chinese Room, the Conservatory, the Yellow Drawing Room, or any of the other rooms which the Regent continued to embellish day after day with new treasures for which he could not afford to pay.

As the Earl, having finished signing his letters, was about to rise from his desk, his secretary, Mr. Stevenson came into the Library.

"Oh, there you are, Stevenson!" the Earl exclaimed. "Cancel all my engagements for the next few days and refuse all these invitations."

"Has your Lordship forgotten you are dining at Carlton House tomorrow evening?" Mr. Stevenson asked respectfully.

"I had, as it happens!" the Earl admitted.

"His Royal Highness will be as mad as fire if we chuck him again," Lord Charles said.

"I cannot help his troubles," the Earl said. "Send a message, Stevenson, to say that urgent family affairs oblige me most regretfully to leave London immediately!"

"That is what you said last time, My Lord."

"Well, say that the house has burnt down or I have a revolution on my hands—anything you like! Nobody is going to stop me from going to the country!"

Mr. Stevenson looked worried, but Lord Charles merely laughed.

"As soon as you get there you will want to come back!"

"Do you want to bet on it?" the Earl enquired.

"Certainly not! It would make you stay longer just to

win, even if it were the last penny I have in my pocket!"

"Very well, no bets!" the Earl said. "But I assure you, I find the country very much more alluring than anything you can offer me in London."

Lord Charles was only half listening.

He walked to the desk from which the Earl had moved and was now scribbling a few lines on a piece of crested writing paper.

He then put it into an envelope, addressed it, and said to Mr. Stevenson:

"Will you have this sent round by hand?"

"Of course, My Lord!"

The Earl took a quick glance at the note as his secretary took it, and there was a faint smile on his lips as he walked through the Hall to where his high-perched Phaeton was waiting outside.

It was a new acquisition that had only recently come from the Coach builders and was drawn by a team of four perfectly matched chestnuts that he had bought the previous year.

They were his favourites and he knew he was going to enjoy driving them to Fleet.

As he picked up the reins he remembered that his record stood at two hours, five minutes.

Lord Charles climbed into the seat beside him, the groom in his cockaded hat jumped up behind, and they moved off.

It was difficult to suppose that any man could drive more expertly than the Earl. He was of course known as a "Corinthian," but he rather despised the title.

They had driven for some way in silence before he said:

"I am glad you are coming with me, Charles. It is

always fun when we are together. At the same time, as I have told you already, I have been feeling somewhat depressed."

"It is no use, Alaric," Lord Charles replied in a more serious tone than he had used hitherto. "One cannot put back the clock and, whatever you may say, we will both of us be thirty-three by the end of the year, and perhaps it is time we settled down."

"How, may I ask?"

"Getting married for one thing!"

The Earl laughed.

"If I have met any marriageable young women in the last two years, I have not been aware of it."

"They have been there, but you have chosen not to notice them," Lord Charles said, "while their mothers are torn between a desire to capture you as a wealthy and desirable son-in-law, and the fear that with your reputation you would ruin the wretched girls' chances just by dancing with her!"

"Good God!" the Earl ejaculated. "You do not mean to say it is as bad as that!"

"It is not far off it," Lord Charles replied, "and who shall blame you? You have everything a man could desire, and the women circle round you like hungry bees round a honey pot!"

The Earl laughed. Then he said:

"I am not sure whether you are being poetical or just damned impertinent!"

"You can take your choice," Lord Charles replied. "And now I think about it, I am sure it is time we did something a bit more sensible and constructive. As far as I am concerned, most of my energy and intelligence is spent just in keeping myself alive!"

"If that is true, then you are being very stupid," the Earl said. "You know I am prepared to share everything I have with you far more willingly than I would share it with some grasping female whom I am expected to 'endow with all my worldly goods.'"

"No one could be more kind," Lord Charles said in a serious voice, "but at my age I should be able to look after myself, although it is very difficult to know how."

"I cannot think what happened to all the money your grandfather had when he was the Duke."

"I can answer that in two words—drink and cards," Lord Charles replied. "He was an inveterate gambler, and one night at Wattier's he lost three Squares and fourteen Streets in the middle of London, and a thousand acres of our best farming land in the country!"

"Your father must have regretted that when he inherited."

"What did he inherit?" Lord Charles asked. "A house that was falling to pieces about our ears, land which is singularly unfertile, and a multitude of debts that we are still paying off year after year with the pittance that was left of what was known as 'a fortune!'"

He spoke bitterly. Then he said:

"Well, I shall never come into it anyway because, as you know, I have two elder brothers. So why should I worry? It is only that I hate to see my parents losing a battle they can never win, and my mother growing increasingly tired and old because she cannot afford enough servants to run the house."

"It is a damnable situation!" the Earl agreed. "Surely you can find some way by which you can make some money?"

"Like what?" Lord Charles asked bitterly.

Then there was silence and the Earl realised there was no answer to that question.

If he had not supported his friend in the Army, it would have been quite impossible for him to find the comparatively large income that was required by an Officer in a smart Cavalry Regiment.

It had therefore been inevitable that when he bought himself out on his father's death, he should pay for Charles to do so too.

Now, although it seemed ridiculous, the Earl thought the future was somewhat grim for both of them, apart from the fact that he had everything that money could buy.

Something within him demanded more.

If he was honest, he knew that his talents, and they were quite considerable, were being wasted, and as his friend had told him, a life of pleasure, of making love to one woman after another, would never satisfy him.

"What do I want? And how can I get it if I do not know what it is?" he asked.

Because there was no easy reply, the two men drove on almost in silence.

As the huge house, Fleet, which was the Earl's ancestral home, came in sight, he took out his watch and looked at it. Then he said with an air of triumph:

"Two hours, three minutes! I believe that is a new record!"

"It certainly is," Lord Charles agreed, "and the only thing to do is to go back tomorrow and try to make it five minutes shorter!"

"I shall do nothing of the sort!"

The Earl looked ahead and thought with satisfaction

that with the sun glinting on its windows, Fleet looked very beautiful.

Originally a Priory, every succeeding Earl had built onto it until in the middle of the last century the present Earl's grandfather when he was an old man had completely changed the appearance of it.

Now there were Ionic pillars supporting a portico above the flight of stone steps that led to the front door.

The original Priory had now lost every vestige of its original appearance and instead was a Georgian gentleman's house in the full sense of the word.

It stood in exquisite gardens laid out by the finest landscape gardener in England, and in front of it was a huge lake over which glided swans both black and white.

The Earl's standard flew from the rooftop, and along the parapet of the roof stood statues of goddesses silhouetted against the blue of the sky.

'It is a house of dreams,' the Earl had often thought to himself, and he never saw it without getting a little thrill because it was his and because in itself it was everything he wanted his home to be.

He was thinking however that ever since he had inherited, his relations had begged him to be married and produce not one heir, but a half dozen of them to make sure of the succession.

"Your father was bitterly disappointed that he had only one child," his Aunts would say as if it were something original. "You must make sure while you are still young that the Nurseries on the top floor are filled so that we need not worry, as we did when you were in the Army, that the Earldom might come to an end."

It seemed extraordinary, the Earl had often thought,

that among his relations there was a great preponderance of daughters. It was as if the family had been cursed in not producing sons.

'It is something I shall have to see about sooner or later,' he thought.

Then he told himself that despite his grumbles he actually enjoyed being in London and found that while there were beautiful women ready and willing to fall into his arms, there was no need for marriage until he was very much older.

He admitted to himself however that Charles was right, and thirty-two was going to seem very old to a young woman of eighteen or nineteen.

He was aware that after that age a girl was either so plain that she was destined to become an old maid, or if she was pretty enough, already married to somebody else.

And yet the mere thought of marriage made him shiver.

He was man enough to accept the favours he was offered. It would have seemed very priggish to refuse the women who gave him their bodies and their hearts without apparently a thought for their husbands.

But the Earl always felt in a strange way that when he humiliated a man by taking his wife into his arms, he was humiliated too.

It was as if, being complacent husbands, they insulted the whole of the male sex, and yet it was indisputedly part of the world in which he lived.

If he had so much as hinted at his real feelings, it would have caused a gale of laughter and scorn from everybody around him.

The Regent as Prince of Wales had set the pace by pursuing a number of beautiful women one after another who inevitably were already married with the exception of Mrs. Fitzherbert, who was a widow.

His marriage with Princess Caroline had proved disastrous and he had returned very quickly to the married women he preferred, whose husbands apparently thought it a privilege for His Royal Highness to desire what was legally theirs.

"I am damned if I would allow my wife to behave in such a way!" the Earl had said to himself a dozen times as he went up the stairs in another man's house to his wife's bed.

Because it had been easier to "swim with the tide" than against it, he did not express such ideas to the women, who either assured him their husbands were no longer interested in them or were conveniently away for a few nights.

In the last year what had been just a casual thought had gradually become a distaste for the intrigue and the feeling when the fires of desire had died down a little that it was all rather cheap and sordid.

As he drew nearer to Fleet he had told himself that he would make sure that any woman he brought there bearing his name would behave herself.

If he ever found her philandering with a man like himself he would strangle her!

Then he thought that if he said such a thing out loud even Charles would not understand and would laugh at him.

Yet as he drew his horses up outside the porticoed front door and the footmen in their smart livery rolled down the red carpet, he knew exactly what he wanted. The only difficulty was that it might be impossible ever to find it.

                              *   *   *

The Earl and Lord Charles were welcomed by the Butler
who was waiting in the Hall and there were four footmen
to take their hats and driving coats from them.

"It's good to see you back, M'Lord!" the Butler said
respectfully. "Luncheon will be ready in ten minutes, if
that's Your Lordship's wish."

Lord Charles was aware that when the Earl had said
he was going to the country a groom from Berkeley
Square had been despatched to alert the household of his
imminent arrival.

It always amused him to see how like clockwork
everything ran smoothly as soon as the Earl appeared.

Champagne on ice was cooled to exactly the right
temperature, the Sitting Room had fresh flowers in the
vases, and the sun blinds were lowered to exactly the
right angle to rest the eyes.

They walked into luncheon in the small Dining Room
which the Earl preferred to use when there was not a
party.

Each dish was an epicurean delight and the wine,
which came from his very extensive cellars beneath the
house, was superb.

The two friends talked of horses for some time during
the meal. Then they talked of the war situation.

Finally when the servants had withdrawn they sat back
comfortably in their chairs, a glass of matured brandy at
their sides and a feel of comfort and satisfaction which
Lord Charles was sure had swept away the irritation and
depression the Earl had shown earlier in the day.

"The first thing we will do," the Earl said, "is to take

out some of the horses I am trying to break in, and get the devil out of them."

"A good idea," Lord Charles agreed. "I expect my riding clothes will have been unpacked by now."

"I will raise hell if they have not!"

"I am only teasing," Lord Charles confessed. "As you are well aware, everything at Fleet is run to perfection, and I cannot imagine there could ever be anything amiss or with which you would find fault."

"I hope you are right," the Earl said, "but I expect my wife, if I ever have one, will find traces of dust somewhere or be ready to find fault even if it is only with the lowliest scullery maid!"

Lord Charles looked at him with a glint of interest in his eyes.

"Are you thinking of taking a wife?"

"I suppose it is something I shall have to do sooner or later!"

"That is not the right way to look at it . . ." Charles began.

As he spoke the door opened and the Butler came into the room.

He walked to the Earl's side and said in a low voice:

"Excuse me, M'Lord, but there's a young lady waiting to see you!"

"A young lady?"

It flashed through the Earl's mind that Oline might have followed him, but quickly decided that was impossible.

She had always said she hated the country, and what was more, however outrageously she might behave in London, she would not risk her social reputation by blatantly proclaiming her feelings in such a manner.

"What name did the young lady give, Newman?" he asked.

"She said, M'Lord, that you would not know her, but she has to see you because it's on a very important subject."

The Earl looked surprised. Then he said:

"Is there any reason why she should be so secretive?"

"I don't know, M'Lord."

"You said a young lady, Newman. Is she a Lady?"

"Definitely, M'Lord!"

"How did she come here?"

"She rode, M'Lord, and alone!"

"Alone?"

The Earl's voice expressed his surprise.

It was unheard of for a Lady—and he knew Newman would never make a mistake about someone's social status—to ride unaccompanied by a groom.

He looked at Charles who was obviously as interested and surprised as he was.

Then the Earl said:

"I expect she has come to ask for money for some local charity or other, or perhaps she wishes to sell me a horse."

"I don't think it's that, M'Lord," Newman said.

"Did she tell you anything else?"

"No, except that it's very important she should see Your Lordship."

The Earl sighed.

"We were just going riding."

"I dare say it will not take long," Lord Charles said, "and it would be extremely irritating if we send her away

24

to find ourselves wondering for the rest of the day what it was all about."

"You are right, Charlie. I will see her in the Library, Newman."

"I've already shown her in there, M'Lord."

Newman went towards the door and the Earl deliberately finished his brandy because he rose.

"I had hoped," he said as he put down his glass, "that we would be able to stay here undisturbed."

"Bees round a honey pot," Lord Charles teased.

The Earl raising his fist punched him lightly on the side of his head as he walked past him to the door.

"You had better come with me, Charlie," he said. "I feel if our lady visitor does not need a chaperon, I do!"

Lord Charles laughed and rising followed the Earl slowly as he walked ahead of him down the corridor.

He had the feeling that his friend, despite his outward reluctance, was quite pleased that something was happening they had not expected.

'Let us hope,' Lord Charles said to himself, 'that whatever this woman has to say is worth listening to!'

chapter two

LORD Milborne, reading the newspaper with his leg raised on a stool in front of him, heard a door open and turned his head expectantly.

There was the sound of footsteps coming across the hall, then his daughter, Salrina, came into the room.

Her eyes looked worried and one glance told him she had brought bad news.

"Well?" he asked uncompromisingly.

"Hewitt cannot do it, Papa," Salrina said. "He is nearly crippled with rheumatism this time, and could hardly let me into the cottage."

"Damnation!" Lord Milborne exclaimed. "That means I lose three hundred guineas!"

"Oh, not as much as that, Papa!" Salrina exclaimed.

She ran across the room to kneel down beside her father's armchair.

"Did you really sell Orion for three hundred guineas?"

"He is worth every penny of it," Lord Milborne said gruffly, "and I am quite certain that Carstairs would have won the Steeplechase on him!"

"Of course he would! But now I suppose we cannot get him there on time."

"How can we?" Lord Milborne asked testily. "Here am I, laid up with this accursed leg, and Hewitt with rheumatism. There is no one else I would trust with Orion, as you well know."

"Except me!"

Her father turned to look at his daughter as if he had never seen her before.

She was very lovely, with a small heart-shaped face that seemed to be filled by two large blue eyes.

She had a tiny, straight, aristocratic nose and her mouth, though not a Cupid's bow, had something irresistibly impish about it.

It was perhaps because she was always laughing, and when she did so, there were two dimples in her soft cheeks.

Now, however, her expression was serious as she looked at her father.

"You know I can manage Orion, he is always good with me, and you cannot afford to lose all that money, Papa."

"That is true," Lord Milborne said almost as if he were speaking to himself. "At the same time, I cannot have you riding all that way alone."

"It is not more than ten miles across country," Salrina said, "and if I start out early I can be back before dark, or very nearly."

"It is impossible!" her father said firmly.

Salrina rose from the side of his chair to walk to the window and stare out onto the unkempt garden which had grown wild since her mother's death.

Lady Milborne had loved flowers and, while her husband was breaking in and training horses which he sold at a profit, she was quite content to make her house as comfortable and the garden as beautiful as she could for him.

They had been what everybody who knew them called "an ideally happy couple," and when she died two winters ago when it was very cold and they could not afford to keep the house properly heated, only Salrina had prevented her father from killing himself because he could not bear to live without the woman he loved.

But Salrina in trying to take her mother's place had found it almost impossible to prevent themselves from running into debt.

The horses brought in quite a lot of money because her father was very skilled at training them.

At the same time they sometimes had their failures, and at the moment everything seemed to have gone wrong.

Lord Milborne had had a bad fall when he was taking a new and wild young horse over the jumps.

While he had not broken his leg, he had sprained it very badly; and it would be impossible for him to ride for at least another two weeks.

The only person he had to help him was Hewitt, who before he became a groom had been a jockey.

He was exceedingly good with horses, but he was getting old and had bouts of what he called his "rheumatics," which gave him not only excruciating pain, but prevented him from moving about, let alone ride.

This meant that for the moment Salrina had to look

after the horses, feed them, exercise them, and do what she could to school them, although her father had absolutely forbidden her to touch any of those that were as yet not broken in.

In addition to her father's accident they were, she knew, in debt once again, and three hundred guineas would be an absolute Godsend and allow them to enjoy a few luxuries for a change.

"It is quite impossible for you to go!" Lord Milborne said as if he were following her thoughts.

"Travis has intimated, Papa, that he cannot allow us to have any more meat unless we settle his account, and Higgs said very much the same yesterday when he delivered feed for the horses."

"Curse it! Why did you not tell me?" Lord Milborne asked angrily.

"Because I knew it would upset you, Papa, and I have thought we could manage for a little longer until you were better."

Lord Milborne was silent.

He knew better than anybody else that if the horses were not properly fed they would take longer to get fit and that would mean a delay in selling them.

There was silence as Salrina turned from the window. Then she said:

"I will leave at six o'clock tomorrow morning, Papa, riding Orion and leading Jupiter on a leading rein. If Orion is skittish, I know I can rely on Jupiter to follow me, even if I cannot lead him."

Lord Milborne was aware this was true, for Jupiter was Salrina's own special horse which she loved and had brought up from the time he was foaled.

It was Salrina who named all the horses that came

into the ramshackle stables that adjoined the small Manor House in which they lived.

Because she loved mythology she always gave them the names of gods and goddesses, and those who habitually dealt with Lord Milborne would laugh and say to him:

"Have you anything especially divine for me today, Milborne? I prefer something as fast as Mercury, if you have it!"

Lord Milborne was still a comparatively young man, having disobeyed his parents and run away when he was at Oxford with a beautiful girl who was engaged to a rich and very important Baronet.

Her parents, like his, had been infuriated by their action, but there was nothing they could do when the eloping couple returned south from Gretna Green.

After five years of stiff silence between the families they were gradually reconciled to the position and accepted it with a bad grace.

This meant as far as Lord Milborne was concerned, that when he inherited the title, he found that his father had left most of his money, which was not a very large sum anyway, to his younger son, while his wife on her father's death received only the capital from which her allowance was paid, which brought in about fifty pounds a year and no more.

They therefore had to scrimp and save every possible penny, but actually Salrina's parents had been blissfully happy together.

Never once in the years they were married had they regretted their elopement which everybody else described as reckless and irresponsible.

Salrina had been born ten months after their marriage

at Gretna Green. While her father regretted he had no son, she could not help thinking it was a blessing that she was, in fact, his only child.

She was sensible enough to realise that while with her mother's help she had educated herself from books, a brother would have expected to go to a Public School and perhaps even to University, and it was impossible to imagine how they would have been able to afford it.

"I am not having you riding over the countryside by yourself, whether it is ten miles or a hundred!" Lord Milborne said as if he were following his own train of thought. "You are too young and too pretty, for one thing, and it is something no Lady would do for another!"

Salrina laughed.

"It is no use, Papa, talking to me as if I were an elegant young Lady of Fashion, having nothing more to do than embroider pretty samplers or occasionally paint a watercolour in the garden. There are six horses waiting for me to feed them at this moment, and as Hewitt cannot muck out the stables, you know I have to help. Poor Len is quite incapable of doing it by himself."

Len was the loonyboy of the village who was perfectly happy to mess about in the stables for a few pence a week.

Because he came from a bad home and was always hungry, Salrina fed him, and it was that more than the money that made him happy at the Manor.

"I do not know what your mother would say," Lord Milborne muttered.

Salrina knew he was weakening and, like her, he was well aware they literally could not afford to lose three hundred guineas.

"But I will not have you coming home in the dark," he went on.

Salrina gave a sudden cry.

"I know what I will do, Papa, which is much more sensible."

"There is nothing whatever sensible about it," Lord Milborne muttered, "but tell me."

"I will arrive at Mr. Carstairs's house in the afternoon, then stay with old Mabel at Little Widicot for the night. I know she would be pleased to see me, and then I can come home quietly the next morning without your worrying about me."

"I shall worry anyway!" Lord Milborne said crossly. "Why I have to be a 'cursed crock' at this particular moment, God only knows!"

Salrina looked at him sympathetically.

Her father seldom swore in front of her and she knew it infuriated him that he should be incapacitated.

At the same time he was extremely worried about her riding alone, even for a short distance.

She was not so foolish, nor so innocent, as not to realise that because she was very like her mother, men were attracted by her.

But up until now there had been only young farmers to look at her in admiration and the choirmen in the Church, and just occasionally her father's customers came to him instead of his going to them.

When that happened they paid her compliments and when they left usually said in her hearing:

"When your daughter grows up, Milborne, you will have to take her to London. I predict she will be the toast of St. James's the moment she appears!"

Lord Milborne had either laughed or not listened.

But this last year, when she was eighteen, Salrina had been aware that when any gentleman of the *Beau Ton* called at the Manor her father either told her to keep out of sight, or sent her on an errand to the village.

Those were his orders, and what usually happened if the visitor stayed for a meal, was that Salrina had to help old Nanny in the kitchen with the cooking.

There was no one else in the house except for her old Nurse who was now nearly seventy and had been in her grandparents' house when her mother was a girl.

When Salrina was born she had come to the Manor to look after her.

She was another person, Salrina knew, who would be horrified at the idea of her riding alone and she would argue about it more fiercely than her father had done.

Nanny was however well aware that if they did not get some money soon they would be on the verge of starvation.

What invariably happened was that because he had to buy the horses to train, cheap though they were, Lord Milborne always spent in advance the miserable income he received from his new shares before it was due.

The Bank had now limited his overdraft to the point where it was a permanent debt.

He knew when he died it would be passed on like a millstone to Salrina.

"Three hundred guineas!" Salrina was saying, then wordlessly a little later when Nanny was repeating over and over again that it was impossible for her to go such a long distance without someone to accompany her.

"The best thing you can do, Nanny, is to come with me yourself!" she said at length.

"There's no use joking about it, Miss Salrina," Nanny answered sharply. "I know what's right, and what your mother'd think was right. You're a young lady, not some hobbledehoy stable lad!"

"I cannot see much difference at the moment," Salrina replied, "and you know as well as I do, Nanny, that we need that three hundred guineas. If Mr. Carstairs does not have Orion in time for the Steeplechase he will not buy him."

Nanny pressed her lips together and Salrina knew she was trying to find an alternative to what she was doing.

But there was none.

To save herself from continual arguments from either Nanny or her father, Salrina went to the stables and brushed Orion down again.

He was a fine-looking bay who Salrina thought was well worth the three hundred guineas her father was getting for him, but it was a much bigger sum than he usually obtained.

But Mr. Carstairs, a pushy, arrogant young man, who had as Nanny said "jumped up in the world," was determined to beat the "Toffs" who had inaugurated the Steeplechase to which he was invited only because it took place on the land he farmed.

Steeplechases were sometimes local events which took place annually, but often they were a pastime for the Bucks and Beaux.

They would come down from London to stay with one of their kind in his ancestral home and think up amusing ways to pass the time.

Salrina had heard talk of wild parties at which beautiful women were often present.

After dinner the gentlemen would race against each

other in the moonlight, sometimes so "foxed" that they fell off their horses at the first fence, injuring themselves because they were in no fit condition to ride.

She had been shocked at such stories, then told herself that they were probably exaggerated simply because in the country there was nothing much to talk about.

Gossip that was passed from person to person therefore became a very different tale by the time it reached her father or her.

Nevertheless, while she did not like Mr. Carstairs and thought him rather coarse, she knew he was a good rider and that the horses in his stables were well looked after.

"You must never, Papa," she had often said to her father, "sell our horses to anyone who is not kind to them. Because you are never cruel they would not understand any other treatment, and I could not bear that any of them should be unhappy."

"I know exactly what you mean," Lord Milborne replied, "and quite frankly, my dearest, if I were a rich man, I would never sell any of my horses."

He was silent for a moment before he went on.

"When one has ridden a horse, even for a short time, it becomes part of oneself, and I care for all mine as if they were my children."

Salrina had understood and had flung her arms around his neck.

"I love you, Papa, and I am sure no other man could be as wonderful or as kind as you! I pray every night that by some miracle you will become a millionaire!"

Her father had laughed.

"That is as likely as that I should own a Racing Stable, or jump over the moon!"

They had laughed together, and watching her father's

patience as he trained the horses with kindness, knowing they were timid and did not understand what was expected of them, she knew she could never tolerate any man who did not understand animals, and especially horses.

*   *   *

The next morning Salrina groomed Orion again, then went into the house to find her father just finishing his breakfast.

He had dressed himself with difficulty, and because he had been restless during the night, his leg was extremely painful.

He looked at his daughter as she came into the room, thinking how very like her mother she was.

She was lovely in the same heartbreaking way that had made him fall in love so completely with her mother at first sight that he had known that nothing and nobody should prevent him from making her his wife.

They must have been meant for each other by Fate or perhaps a benign Providence for Elizabeth Layton had felt exactly the same about him.

From the moment she looked at his handsome face she had known no other man should ever touch her.

"If the Prince of Wales had gone down on his knees before me," she had told Gavin Borne, "I would not have hesitated for one moment if you had wanted me to."

"Want you?" he had replied. "You are mine, Elizabeth, mine completely and absolutely, and I swear no other man shall ever have you!"

He had kissed her passionately and they had run away a week later.

It had been a long, arduous, and sometimes uncomfortable journey to get to Gretna Green.

However they had enjoyed every moment of it, and after they had married, Elizabeth Borne had lived in a very special Heaven where nothing mattered except her husband, and later her daughter, Salrina.

"Are you quite sure, Mama, you did not regret giving up the Balls and the comfort in which you lived for Papa?" Salrina had asked once.

Her mother had laughed and the sound was like a peal of bells.

"How can you ask such a foolish question?" she said. "I have everything—everything any woman could want: the most handsome, adorable husband in the whole world, and a very lovely sweet little daughter. Oh, Salrina, I am so lucky!"

The way she spoke was so sincere that Salrina had felt the tears come into her eyes.

She had known then that what her mother had told her all the years she had been growing up was true, and that the only thing that mattered in life was love.

Nothing else was of any consequence.

It was Nanny who grumbled after her mother's death and said in her frank manner:

"I don't know what's going to happen to you, that I don't!"

"What do you mean by that, Nanny?" Salrina had asked.

"Living here, seeing no one and going nowhere. You'll grow up, Miss Salrina, and where are you going to find a husband, I'd like to know?"

"I do not want a husband at the moment. I am perfectly happy with Papa," Salrina replied.

"All you both think about is horses!" Nanny said snappily. "It may be all right for your father, but you'll be wanting to be married in a year or two, and you can't marry a horse!"

Salrina had laughed and teased Nanny by saying she would rather marry Jupiter than any man she had ever met or heard of.

But sometimes at night when she could not sleep she would wonder whether there was anything more in life for her than training horses which, when she had grown to love them, were sold.

Then like her father she would have to start all over again with another horse.

Although she tried not to grow too fond of them because it made her unhappy when they went away, she found it impossible not to love them.

When they nuzzled with their noses against her she felt as if she meant something special to them and it gave her a warm feeling inside.

'Perhaps it would be the same if one loved a man,' she told herself.

But since there was nobody to whom she could talk about it, she just tried to make her father happy, being aware how desperately he missed her mother, as she did.

Now as Lord Milborne looked at his daughter there was an expression of pain in his eyes because in her riding habit which was old and slightly threadbare and had belonged to her mother she looked so like her.

She was also wearing her mother's riding hat with its high crown and a piece of pale blue gauze round it which floated out behind as she moved.

Beneath her jacket she wore a white blouse, and the lace of a stiff starched petticoat showed beneath her skirt.

She certainly looked very much smarter than she did any other day.

She also seemed older, and there was now a look of apprehension on Lord Milborne's face that told Salrina even before he spoke that he was going to be difficult.

"I am ready now, Papa," Salrina said, "and before you start saying all over again that it is something I should not do, I promise you I will not stay one moment longer with Mr. Carstairs after I have handed over Orion and, I hope, received his cheque. Then I will ride without speaking to anybody else straight to Mabel's cottage."

Mabel was an old woman who had kept a shop in the village for years.

She had adored Lady Milborne, and one of Salrina's earliest memories was being given lollipops by "Mabel," as she was always known in the village.

She had kept the shop until her son had wanted to take it over, and she had then moved into his cottage which was at Little Widicot, on the Earl of Fleetwood's estate, for whom he worked.

"The village will not seem the same without Mabel!" Lady Milborne had often said.

Whenever she had time to spare she would ride over to see her in her cottage, and sometimes Salrina would accompany her on her pony.

"Mabel will not only be pleased to see me, Papa," Salrina went on before her father could speak, "but she will ask a thousand questions about you and will be very distressed to hear that you have injured your leg."

"Not half as distressed as I am," Lord Milborne replied. "But listen, Salrina, I have been thinking about your journey."

Salrina waited, thinking there was nothing more than

40

she had said already to convince him she would not get into any trouble.

Then he surprised her.

"Because, as you are aware, this is something you should not do," he said, "if by any chance anyone should ask your name, you are not to say who you are."

Salrina's eyes opened wide.

"Why not, Papa?"

"Because it would be very bad for your reputation if it became known in the County or anywhere else that you rode without being accompanied by a groom or a chaperon."

"I understand," Salrina agreed.

She was in fact relieved that her father had not started the argument as to whether she should or should not go all over again.

"I can easily call myself something other than Milborne," she said. "What do you suggest?"

"Think of anything you like," her father said in an irritated voice, "but I will not have people talking about you, do you understand?"

Salrina longed to reply that she did not think there was anyone to talk, or if he was thinking of the sort of people to whom it would matter, they would either not be interested enough or have no idea that her father was a Lord.

She was not so half-witted that she did not realise that if they could have afforded the expense at her age she would have been presented to the King and Queen at Buckingham Palace.

She would have been invited to attend Balls, Assemblies, and functions of every sort as a Society débutante.

There were very few, as it happened, large houses in

their neighborhood, and the ones there were inhabited by elderly people who seldom entertained and had in fact taken little, if any, notice of Lord and Lady Milborne, who could not afford to invite them back.

It was only shortly before her mother died that she had said occasionally:

"I wish we had one smart relation who would have you to stay in London, or even give a Ball for you in the country."

"Where are all our relatives?" Salrina had asked.

"That is something I often ask myself," her mother had replied. "Your father's brother, the rich one of the family, is a very distinguished soldier, but he is at the moment, as you know, fighting with Wellington's Army."

She paused, then added quickly:

"But do not talk about him in front of Papa, dearest, because it upset him that he cannot fight too, as he would like to do."

"Why not?" Salrina had asked the first time her mother had said this.

"Because," Lady Milborne had explained, "he could hardly leave you and me here alone to starve, and actually I thank God every night that we are too poor for him to leave me."

There was a little throb in her voice and a suspicion of tears in her eyes which told Salrina how terrified her mother would have been if her father had insisted upon being a soldier.

She now understood that her mother, while she was utterly and completely content with her life as it was, wanted more for her daughter.

She also understood what her father was trying to say and she replied:

"Do not worry, Papa. I will forget I am the 'Honourable' which as far as I am concerned is not worth a penny in the open market, and if anybody asks me who I am, I will say that my name is Milton, which is near enough to yours for me to remember it, and I have just been reading *Paradise Regained!*"

Her father laughed.

"Perhaps that is what you and I will find together when you come back with the three hundred guineas!"

"Exactly, Papa! And we will have a feast the first night I bring it back and pay Mr. Travers what we owe him. In fact, while I am handing Orion over I will be wondering whether you would enjoy most a large beefsteak, a leg of lamb, or a piece of tender veal."

"I will decide that while you are away." Her father smiled.

He held out his arms as he spoke and Salrina kissed him affectionately on both cheeks.

"Take care of yourself, dearest Papa," she admonished him, "and remember you are not to put any pressure on your leg at all or it will take that much longer to heal."

"You are bullying me, as usual!" her father complained. "But I shall miss you, so hurry back to me tomorrow."

He held on to her for a moment as he said:

"Swear to me that you will take care of yourself! I know in my heart I should not let you go."

"You are not to worry," Salrina said lightly, "and if I am in trouble I am quite sure Mama will be looking after me."

She saw her father's expression change and as usual when they spoke of his wife there was a tenderness in his eyes.

Salrina ran from the room, looking back from the door only to wave to her father before she made her way to the stables.

Orion was ready for her in the stall where she had left him, and Len, looking more vacant than usual, was holding Jupiter by his leading rein.

The horse was cropping some of the weeds that had grown up through the cobbles in the yard.

He raised his head when Salrina approached and would have moved towards her if Len had not prevented him from doing so.

Salrina stopped and patted him.

"You are coming with me," she said, "and you have to be very good and helpful."

She felt as if he almost understood, because she always talked to him.

She glanced up to see if all the things she needed for the night were safely strapped to his saddle.

The stirrup was turned up on the side saddle because she would not be riding him until they returned, and everything else seemed to be in order before she went into the stable to bring out Orion.

He was moving restlessly, bucking a little and tossing his head to show his independence.

She climbed onto the mounting block and held him while she seated herself in the saddle and managed without any help to arrange the fullness of her skirt.

Then she reached out her hand for Jupiter's leading rein, taking it from Len and saying as she did so:

"Good bye, Len! Feed all the horses as I have shown you, and be sure they have enough water before you go home tonight."

"Aye, Miss Salrina," Len said.

His speech was slow and he often stammered and was inarticulate, but he tried to do what Salrina told him.

She had actually already seen that the horses had plenty of food and had filled up their water buckets herself first thing this morning.

She rode down the overgrown drive that led to the Manor, feeling as she did so that in a way this was an adventure.

It was certainly the first time she had ever been away from home on her own, and it was very exciting to be riding Orion and keeping him under control.

She knew she would enjoy even more the ride back on Jupiter, when he would do exactly what she wanted.

Outside the gate she passed through a small village, and as everybody knew Salrina, the women smiled and bobbed a little curtsy, while the men and boys touched their caps or pulled their forelocks as she went by.

She was well aware that by this time everybody would have learnt that she was taking a horse to be sold because her father was unable to take him himself.

She guessed that, because it would be something to talk about, two or three of the older women would pop up to see Nanny during the afternoon to see if her father wanted anything in particular fetched from the shop.

'They are all very kind to us,' Salrina thought to herself.

She knew it was because her father and mother had always shown to whoever it might be kindness and understanding.

She realized exactly what her mother meant to them after her death, for when she was buried in the Churchyard, not only on the day of the Funeral, but for weeks afterwards there were small bunches of flowers on her grave.

At Christmas there had been wreaths made of holly and mistletoe that had no name on them, but came from the simple people of the village who had loved her as she had loved them.

Orion shied at a sheep grazing by the roadside, and Salrina had to think of him rather than of her mother or herself.

Although she thought she knew the way to Mr. Carstairs's house, she found it more difficult than she had expected, because going across country she tried to avoid gates to open, as she did not wish to dismount from Orion.

This would have meant loosing Jupiter, and for the same reason she also wanted to avoid having to jump any hedges. The detours she therefore had to make took longer than she expected.

Then unexpectedly the sun went in and the clouds became dark, and finally it began to thunder.

At the first roll of it Orion pricked up his ears and Salrina knew that he was alert and nervous.

Most animals, she knew, disliked thunderstorms, although she had never had any trouble with Jupiter.

Now she thought it would be very difficult if Orion bolted or, worse still, refused to proceed any farther.

She knew her father had trained horses who became static in storms and would not move from under a tree, or even eat their food, if they were frightened by thunder and lightning.

The rolls of thunder came nearer and as she anticipated, Orion played up at every one.

Somehow she persuaded him to go forward, until to her consternation she realised that she had lost her way, was not certain where she was, while the sky was growing darker every minute.

It was obvious there was going to be a heavy fall of rain.

It arrived about five minutes later with a force that made Salrina know they had to take shelter.

With the greatest difficulty she managed to make Orion move in the opposite direction to which they had been going because the rain was beating down behind them rather than straight into their faces.

Then to her relief she saw that just across the field over which they were riding was a Posting Inn.

It was not a very important one, but it was an Inn and she knew with a sense of relief that there would be stables.

As there was no barn of any sort where they could shelter, she thought her father would approve if she put the horses in stables at the Inn until the storm was over.

Again with a great deal of difficulty because Orion disliked not only the rumbles overhead, and the rain beating down on his head, she quickly rode into the yard.

There appeared to be nobody about and she saw the stables on one side and the Inn on the other.

Because Orion was now rearing up in protest against the elements she released Jupiter's rein and took him hastily in through the nearest stable door.

There was a horse in the stall exactly opposite her, but there was another stall to the left of it that was empty and to her joy another empty stall was beyond that.

There was no sign of an ostler and she quickly pulled

Orion into the first empty stall and shut him in, then fetched Jupiter, who was waiting patiently outside in the rain.

"You are a very good boy!" she said to him as she led him into the other stall.

It was obvious the rain would continue for some time and now it appeared to be pouring down as if the Heavens themselves had opened.

She therefore took off Jupiter's bridle and saw there was hay in the manger and water in a somewhat battered pail beside it.

She patted his neck to show him how pleased she was with his good behaviour and carrying the bridle out of the stall hung it on a hook on the wall.

Then she went to Orion.

She realised as she entered his stall again that it was rather larger than Jupiter's, and somebody had obviously that morning thrown down some fresh straw.

This was a relief because some Posting Inns were dirty, and she had no wish after all the trouble she had taken for Orion to arrive at Mr. Carstairs's not looking worth the money he was paying for him.

She removed Orion's bridle also, and hung it too on a hook beside Jupiter's, then went to the door to wonder if she should go into the Posting Inn to explain her presence.

She then noticed through the rain that in the centre of the yard there was a Phaeton.

It was a fashionable one with high wheels, and she glanced back and saw there was not only a horse in the first stall inside the door but another in the stall beyond it.

Now that she had time to inspect them she realised they were well-bred and must belong to a Gentleman of

Fashion, who, like herself, was sheltering from the rain.

She thought for a minute, then knew that if she went inside the Inn to tell the Proprietor she had taken advantage of his stables without asking permission, she might become involved with gentlemen of whom her father would not approve.

And although it seemed ridiculous, he would imagine they would constitute some kind of danger to her.

She thought it over for a minute and told herself the best thing she could do in the circumstances was to stay in the stables until the rain stopped.

If nobody came to question her presence she could then ride away without anybody being aware of her very existence.

It certainly seemed the easiest thing to do, and she looked round for somewhere to sit while she waited.

There was however nothing on which she could seat herself, and she thought it would not be very dignified if anyone found her on the floor, while it would be tiring to stand propped against the walls for perhaps an hour.

She was also aware that she was damp from the rain and she thought it would be a good idea to remove her riding jacket before the dampness soaked through to her blouse beneath it.

Accordingly, because it seemed to be the only place available, she went back into Orion's stall.

The fresh straw had been piled higher on one side than the other, as if actually it had been stacked there to use elsewhere.

There was plenty of room for Salrina to sit down on the straw and not interfere with Orion, who was eating the hay in the manger and merely pricked up his ears as she joined him.

Taking off her jacket, Salrina laid it down beside her on the straw to dry and settle down with her back against the partition between the two stalls, thinking it would be pleasant if she could have a cup of tea.

Nanny had given her a sandwich before she had left home, insisting that she needed it because she had had such an early breakfast.

She was, therefore, not hungry but rather thirsty, and she wondered if she should drink some of Orion's water, but the pail was as dented and dilapidated as the one in Jupiter's stall and she decided against it.

She was quite comfortable, half-lying on the softness of the fresh straw and the only sound was of the rain beating on the roof and the movements of four horses.

She did not know how it happened, but she fell asleep.

*   *   *

Salrina awoke to hear a man's voice say:

"Well, thank the Lord this damned rain has stopped! Now you will be able to get on, and for God's sake do not make a mess of it!"

"You need not be afraid of that, *Monsieur!* I promise you I am very experienced."

Hazily, as if she were still dreaming, Salrina heard their voices.

Then with a start of surprise she realised that the man who had just spoken had a French accent.

chapter three

LISTENING intently, Salrina heard a low laugh. Then the Englishman said:

"I am laughing at the way you express it."

"The Emperor, I assure you, *Monsieur,* is very satisfied, and I have never failed yet in an assignment," the Frenchman replied in a slightly affronted tone.

"That is what I have heard," the Englishman answered, "but this, as you know, is such an important one that we cannot contemplate failure."

"There will be no failure, *Monsieur.*"

"Very well then. As soon as the rain stops you had better be on your way to London. You have the address, and your invitation will be waiting for you. Do not forget it, as you will not be allowed into Carlton House without it."

"I understand, *Monsieur.*"

"And do not forget either," the Englishman said in a somewhat dictatorial manner, "that your excuse for speaking to the Prince is to give him a present from the *Marquis* St. Cloud who is unfortunately too ill to accept his hospitality."

"You are certain that the *Marquis* will not decide to be present? If he did, *quel désastre!*"

"I know, I know!" the Englishman said in an irritated tone. "All that has been taken care of. The *Marquis*, I assure you, will be far too ill that evening to attend any party, least of all the one you will be at!"

The Englishman must have looked out through the door because he then said in a different tone:

"The storm is practically over. Get your horses and the sooner you are off the better. It is unfortunate that there were travellers in the Inn, which I did not expect, but they were of no consequence, and as we did not talk in front of them, they will not remember you."

"I sincerely hope not, *Monsieur.*"

The Frenchman must have opened the door of the stall next to Orion. As he did so, he exclaimed:

"*Tiens!* There were no other horses in here when I arrived!"

Instinctively, as if somebody warned her that what she had overheard was dangerous, Salrina slipped farther down on the straw, as she had been a few minutes earlier when she had been asleep.

She shut her eyes and even as she did so she realised that the men who had been talking were now standing outside Orion's stall looking through the barred door.

Then in a whisper the Frenchman said:

"*Une femme!* Do you think she heard what we said?"

52

There was silence after he had spoken, as if the Englishman were considering it. Then he said:

"No, as you can see, she is fast asleep. But we should have taken more care! I saw your Phaeton was the only one in the yard, and I had no idea there might be anybody else in the stables."

"Mais, you sure *elle dort?"* the Frenchman asked.

Because he was agitated his accent was more noticeable and he used more French words than he had previously.

"She is asleep!" the Englishman said firmly. "I will send my groom from where my carriage is sheltering to help the ostler, if he can be found, to put your horses between the shafts. Then I will leave before you do. I have no wish for anybody to see us together."

"Non, non, of course not, *Monsieur!"*

The Englishman walked towards the door, but before he reached it the Frenchman cried hastily:

"There is something I must have, Milord!"

"What is it?"

"The money!"

"Good God, I nearly forgot. Of course, I have it with me."

The Englishman moved back, as if he wanted concealment for what he was doing, and Salrina knew he went into the stall next to hers and the Frenchman followed him.

She did not open her eyes although she was sure no one was now watching her through the barred door.

Very gently, so as not to rustle the straw, she turned and put her eye to one of the many cracks in the partition between the two stalls.

It was far lighter in the next stall than it was in Orion's, for the simple reason that it was opposite the open door into the yard.

She could see quite clearly two men, and the older one, who was grey at the temples, was counting into the other man's hand a number of what she thought were ten pound or twenty pound notes.

He looked rather debauched, she thought, with dark lines under his somewhat protruding eyes, and several double chins above his high cravat.

The other man, who was taking the money in thin, long-fingered, nervous hands, was so typically French that she thought he might have been a caricature of the Dandies she had seen in the cartoons that her father sometimes showed her.

He was thin and wiry with dark eyes, a long nose, and a somewhat foxy look about him.

"One thousand pounds," the Englishman said in a low voice, "and you will have the other thousand as soon as the Regent is dead. With what undoubtedly the Emperor will give you in addition, you will not do badly."

"Merci, Monsieur!"

There was no further comment as the crackling notes went inside the pocket of the Frenchman's smartly cut coat.

"Good-bye, and good luck!" the Englishman said.

Just in case he should look again to see if she was asleep, Salrina lay back in the same position as before and shut her eyes.

It was fortunate she did so, for a few seconds later she realised that the Frenchman was staring at her through the iron bars.

She forced herself to relax as she had done before, as if she were completely exhausted.

And yet she knew perceptively that he was considering whether for safety's sake, he should kill her.

Then she heard him pull at the stall door and as she felt her whole body contract with fear, a voice said:

"T'Master said Oi should 'elp ye, Sir."

The Frenchman turned away.

"Thank you. Now that the rain has stopped I can continue on my journey."

"Very nasty storm, Sir!"

The groom did not wait for a reply but started to lead out the horse from the stall next to Salrina.

The Frenchman followed him with his other horse, and Salrina could hear them putting the horses between the shafts of the Phaeton.

She still lay exactly where she was, knowing it would be very foolish to move. Perhaps the Frenchman would come back to make sure once again that she had not overheard the conversation.

At the same time she held her breath.

She knew that never in her life had she been nearer to death than she had been a few minutes ago.

Then as she waited tense and terrified she heard the groom say:

"Thank ye, Sir, thank ye!"

A minute later she heard his footsteps as he ran from the courtyard.

The Frenchman in the Phaeton however did not move and Salrina remembered that the Englishman had said that he would leave first.

Faintly in the distance she heard wheels, then a moment or so later there was the clatter of hoofs on the cobbled courtyard as the Frenchman drove his horses onto the road.

Only when she could no longer hear any sound did Salrina jump up, put on her riding jacket and hat, and fetch first Jupiter's bridle from where she had hung it, then Orion's.

When finally they were both ready and she could lead them out into the yard, the sun was shining weakly although everything was dripping from the heaviness of the storm.

She wondered if she should pay for the shelter she had managed to obtain for herself and her horses.

Then she gussed that as the Inn was a small one, and the Englishman had said there were other travellers inside, the ostler would be engaged in serving them.

As he had not helped the Frenchman he would, like the Landlord, be unaware of her.

'The sooner I get away the better!' she thought.

She hurried out onto the road and now looking around she saw a signpost that told her she was, in fact, nearer than she had thought to where Mr. Carstairs lived.

She made no attempt to take to the fields, but following a twisting lane she suddenly saw in front of her the huge ornamental gates surmounted by heraldic stone unicorns, which she knew was the entrance to Fleet.

She had seen it first a long time ago when she had been out riding with her father and several times later when she had come with her mother to visit Mabel.

Little Widicot was in fact less than two miles farther on.

Because she was eager to make up the time she had

lost, she hurried past the white thatched cottages with their gardens bright with spring flowers and put the horses into a quick trot for the last part of the journey.

Mr. Carstairs's farmhouse was well-built and in good condition.

She was not looking forward to seeing him because the last time she had met him he had looked at her in what she thought was an impertinent manner, and she was quite certain he was the type of young man she should avoid, if possible.

It was therefore with a great sense of relief that Salrina, when she rode into the stable yard, found there was only a boy to be seen, carrying two pails of water, but no sign of Mr. Carstairs.

"I have brought the horse your Master is expecting," Salrina said, dismounting from Orion.

"That stall be ready fer 'e," the boy replied.

"If you will show me where it is I will put him in for you, and unsaddle him."

Slowly the boy put down the buckets he was carrying and opened the stable door.

"Th'Master leaves a letter fer whoever brings th' 'orse," he said slowly.

Salrina felt her heart leap. She was sure this contained the three hundred guineas she was hoping to receive.

The boy took the letter from a ledge and held it out to her and she put it into the pocket of her jacket.

She had let Jupiter loose in the yard, knowing he would not wander, and she led Orion into his new stall.

It was very much more luxurious than the one he had had at home, and very much better than the one in which they had sheltered at the Inn.

She knew, however unpleasant she personally might find Mr. Carstairs, his horses were well housed and well looked after.

She removed Orion's bridle and undid the girths of his saddle.

She thought the stable boy might have stayed to help her with the latter, but he had disappeared, so she merely put them outside the stall and went back to pat Orion just in case he felt nervous.

He was already eating the good food in the manger which Salrina noticed was of better quality than they could afford.

"You will be all right, my boy," she said, "and mind you, win the Steeplechase!"

Orion pricked up his ears when she spoke to him, but he was too busy to nuzzle against her and Salrina felt a little pang of unhappiness because she was parting with an animal she had known and ridden for over a year.

He was one of the finest examples of horse flesh her father had ever trained.

She patted Orion again, then went back into the yard where Jupiter was waiting for her.

She undid the leading rein and put it into a pocket of the saddle. Then taking him to the mounting block she seated herself and set off down the track that led from the farm back to the road.

As she did so she felt almost as if somebody had fired a pistol at her and she had to do something about what she had overheard.

Because she had been so frightened that the Frenchman might kill her she had been intent primarily on getting safely away and making up for lost time. So she had not until now really considered the full impact of what she had learnt.

Now as Jupiter carried her smoothly and comfortably towards the village where Mabel's cottage lay, she realised as though seeing it written in letters of fire that the Frenchman had been paid to kill the Regent.

It seemed so incredible, so overtheatrical, that she told herself she must have been mistaken and what she had heard could only be a joke.

Then she went back over the conversation she had listened to, spoken in very low voices with something surreptitious about them because the men were afraid of being overheard.

She knew it actually was a dastardly plot, obviously thought up by the archenemy of England, the Emperor Napoleon Bonaparte, and shamefully connived at by an Englishman.

"How can it be possible that such a thing could happen in London and at Carlton House?" she asked herself.

And yet when she thought of what had been said it all sounded so simple.

The Frenchman had been provided with an invitation and a present from the *Marquis* St. Cloud, who Salrina suspected as one of the many *émigrés* now in England.

Some of these had come in immediately after the French Revolution, but she was aware there had also been others in the last years who loathing the new Régime in France had escaped across the Channel to throw themselves on the mercy of the English.

Her mother had often spoken of their plight and it was only now that Salrina realised that while there were many French people who would be welcome as guests at Carlton

House, it would be possible for an assassin to infiltrate without anybody being aware of it.

The more she thought about it, the more she realised that it was not only possible that His Royal Highness the Prince Regent would be assassinated at his own party, but that she was the one person who could warn him of it.

'If I am, what can I do?' she wondered.

She thought at first that the best thing would be to ride home as quickly as possible and tell her father.

Then she knew that in the predicament he was in at the moment, being incapable of riding, it would agitate and upset him.

The only thing he could do when he learned what she had overheard would be to send her the next morning at the earliest to see the Lord Lieutenant of the County.

He lived nearly as far from her home as she was now, and it was quite easy to calculate that by the time he could reach London to warn His Royal Highness it would be too late.

"What can I do? What can I do?" Salrina asked aloud.

Hearing her voice, Jupiter made a little movement with his head as if he thought she was asking him, but there was no answer.

As they drew nearer to the first house in the outskirts of the village Salrina rode a little slower.

How could she go to Mabel's cottage, sit down and gossip with her about everything she had done since she saw her last, knowing that a Frenchman was on his way to London, intent on killing the handsome, elegant and much-talked-about Prince Regent?

'I have to do something!'

But again the question was—what?

Then as she saw Mabel's cottage ahead of her she also saw above the trees in the Park a flag flying in the breeze.

It was the standard of the Earl of Fleetwood.

She was aware as she saw it silhouetted against the sky that it meant he was at home.

Suddenly, as if it were the answer to her question, she knew what she must do.

If she told the Earl what she had overheard, he had every facility for reaching the Prince Regent quickly to inform him of what had been plotted to happen at his party the next night.

But still Salrina hesitated, knowing that her father would have no wish for her to meet the Earl, who she had heard talked about ever since she had been a child.

He was the most important, the wealthiest, and the most attractive young man in the whole neighbourhood.

Salrina had therefore often heard him being discussed not only by her father and mother and their friends, but also by the farmers, the cottagers, and in fact everybody who lived within talking distance of Fleet.

She had always longed to see the house, but had never had the opportunity.

Her father and mother many years ago when she was tiny had been invited to the garden parties that took place at Fleet once a year.

That was before the late Earl had died and when his son was abroad in the Army.

After he inherited the title the new Earl had made no attempt to entertain the local people.

There was however gossip about the parties he gave where beautiful ladies and distinguished gentlemen came down from London to stay for a few days.

On those occasions there had been races and Steeple-chases in which her father was not invited to take part.

The last one had taken place two months ago, and Lord Milborne had been annoyed because he thought that if he had been invited and had ridden Orion, he would have had a chance, not of winning, but certainly of coming in second or third.

"If I could have shown off his paces," he said bitterly, "I could get a better price for him."

"It is very unkind of the Earl not to ask you, Papa," Salrina had said angrily.

Her father had then shrugged his shoulders and said good-humouredly:

"Why should he? I am of no account in his life, and with the huge sums he pays for his horses he is never likely to be one of my customers."

Salrina knew her father had not given it another thought.

At the same time she felt that the Earl was not behaving as a gentleman should towards his neighbours.

'If Papa were in his position,' she thought, 'he would feel a responsibility to those who lived in the shadow of such an important and magnificent house.'

She would not have been human if she had not wondered what it would be like to be a guest at one of the evening parties the Earl gave.

They were described with relish by the countrywomen who would, she knew, walk miles when they knew the Earl had a party arriving.

They would watch his guests roll through the huge ornamental gates in their elegant carriages and drive down the oak-tree-lined drive to his house over which his standard would be flying.

Sometimes in the last year when she had time she would tell herself a story of how in a beautiful gown and with flowers in her hair she would go to a Ball and dance under huge candlelit chandeliers to the music of a string orchestra.

But there was usually no time for daydreaming because there was so much to do looking after her father and the horses and at night she was so tired that she fell asleep the minute her head touched the pillow.

Fleet had, however, always been an enchanted background for her dreams and now, if she had the courage, she would actually see it for the first time.

When she reached the gates she pulled Jupiter to a standstill and wondered if she was making a mistake.

She had the feeling her father would be furious at her for visiting the Earl on her own.

And yet what was the alternative?

She could hardly send Mabel to tell him a second-hand story of what had occurred.

Even if the old woman was capable of walking down the long drive, would she be listened to by the Butler who opened the door to her?

Would he bother to relay such a fantastic and unlikely tale to his master?

Salrina sighed.

'Something has got to be done, and it is obvious that I shall have to do it myself!' she thought. 'But what will Papa say?'

Then she remembered he had told her that on no account was she to give her real name to anybody.

"I am Miss Milton," Salrina murmured, "and all I have to do is to make the Earl realise he must go to London and save the Prince Regent. Then I can go back to Papa first thing in the morning with an easy conscience."

She rode Jupiter forward and as the gates were open she did not have to shout for the lodge keeper. She guessed it was because the Earl was in residence and was perhaps expecting guests.

Salrina felt a little quiver of fear that if they were smart, fashionable people from London they might laugh her to scorn and she would be turned ignominiously away for talking a lot of nonsense.

Then sensibly she told herself that if that happened no one could blame her if the Prince Regent was, in fact, murdered although she had warned the Earl about the plot.

It was up to him whether he believed her or not.

Then as she saw the house ahead of her she realised it was more magnificent, more breathtaking, and indeed more beautiful than anything she had imagined in her dreams.

It was not only that it was so impressive but there was something, she thought, which made it appear enchanted.

As Jupiter carried her on, she missed nothing of the sunlight glittering like diamonds on hundreds of windows, the silver of the lake, with its black and white swans and the exquisite architecture of the bridge over it which had existed since the days that Fleet had been a Priory.

The sweep in front of the steps that led up to the front door and the gardens that lay on either side of the house were so tidy and so perfect that Salrina felt it was impossible to think of them in the same category as the wilderness at home which was also called a garden.

As she approached she saw a groom come running from one side of the house and knew that this was part of the perfection of His Lordship's domain in which even a casual visitor was immediately attended to by a servant.

As she drew Jupiter to a standstill the groom was already at his head, and having dismounted Salrina said:

"I do not expect to be long, but I would be grateful if my horse could have a drink of water. We have come quite a distance."

"Oi'll see t'it, Ma'am," the groom replied respectfully, and led Jupiter away as Salrina turned towards the steps.

She had only just time to walk up them when the door was opened, and a quick glance told her there was a Butler waiting for her, flanked by four footmen.

She had a sudden feeling of panic and fervently wished she had not come, but left things as they were.

Then almost as if her mother were helping her she knew she could not rest or sleep if her silence resulted in the death of the most important man in the country.

It was therefore in a voice that was soft and yet at the same time quite composed that she said:

"I would like to see the Earl of Fleetwood, please."

"You have an appointment, Madam?"

"I am afraid not, but will you inform His Lordship that it is of the utmost importance that I should speak to him?"

There was, as she expected, quite an argument between her and the Butler before finally he showed her across a marble hall decorated with stone statues into what she thought was a very luxurious and beautiful Sitting Room.

Because she was frightened it was difficult, even when

she was alone, to take in everything around her.

And yet she could not help thinking this was something she would want to remember, and it would be a mistake not to notice there was a very fine Rubens on one wall and a beautiful Poussin on the other.

Lady Milborne had been brought up in a house filled with pictures which had been entailed onto one generation after another.

She had therefore made sure that her daughter's education included an appreciation of painting as well as a knowledge of silver, furniture, and porcelain.

After her mother's death her father had seldom talked to Salrina about anything except horses, but she knew she could never forget what she had learned from her beloved mother.

Now it gave her a pain in her breast to know that she could not go home and describe to her mother what she had seen, so that they could talk it over together and she would learn more about the artists than she had before.

She thought, although she was not sure, that there was a Rembrandt, although quite a small one, between two magnificently gold mirrors that she was sure had been designed by Chippendale.

Then when she was still looking around her the door opened and she stiffened.

She knew that the man who walked in could be nobody but the Earl of Fleetwood.

Never had she expected that any man could look so handsome, so elegant, and yet at the same time aggressively masculine.

He was followed by another man as tall as he was and also good-looking.

Salrina was instantly aware that the Earl's personality seemed to overwhelm her so that it was difficult to look at him and even more difficult to look away.

"You wished to see me?" he asked.

There seemed to be a somewhat contemptuous note in his voice, as if he thought it was a tiresome thing for her to have done.

She curtsied.

"Yes, My Lord, and I must apologise for my intrusion, but it is in fact very important."

"I hope it will not take long," the Earl said sharply, "as I am going riding."

"I am sorry to incommode Your Lordship," Salrina replied, "and I will be as quick as I possibly can."

She hesitated, then she said:

"Perhaps I should see Your Lordship alone?"

She knew as she spoke it was the wrong thing to have said, and she thought there was a definite note of sarcasm in the Earl's voice as he replied:

"Anything you have to say to me, however personal, can be said in front of my friend—Lord Charles Egham."

It was an introduction, and Salrina dropped a little curtsy.

At the same time she did not miss the words "however personal," and she knew that she had been right in thinking the Earl was contemptuous of whatever she had to say to him.

It made her very nervous and it flashed through her mind that the easiest thing she could was to leave and say nothing.

Then, as if Lord Charles understood better than the Earl that she was afraid, he said:

"I should have thought, Alaric, that however much

of a hurry you are in, we might sit down and hear what this lady has to tell us."

"I suppose so," the Earl conceded.

He indicated a chair that was just behind Salrina and she sank down into it, feeling for the moment that her legs would no longer support her.

The Earl seated himself in a high-backed chair on the other side of the hearth rug while Lord Charles lounged back on a comfortable sofa facing them.

She knew they were waiting and after a moment in a voice that sounded to her weak and rather foolish Salrina began.

"You may think it very strange that I have come to see you when I am a stranger, but I do not know what else to do . . . and I am very afraid if I do not tell . . . somebody what has happened the consequences may be very serious."

"Suppose before we go any further you tell us your name?" the Earl suggested.

"Salrina . . . Milton."

There was a definite pause between her first and second name because for one terrifying moment she could not remember what she had decided to call herself.

"Very well, Miss Milton—continue!" the Earl said.

She thought he was making it very difficult and as if Lord Charles understood he said:

"As you have obviously been riding, Miss Milton, and perhaps for a long distance, could we offer you something to drink? A glass of wine, perhaps?"

"No, no . . . nothing, thank you," Salrina said quickly. "I am not really thirsty. It is just that I am so . . . frightened of what may happen."

"You have been ambushed, I imagine, by a High-wayman," the Earl said, "and that, may I say, is a complaint which should be taken to the Chief Constable and not to me!"

"No, My Lord, it is . . . nothing like that."

The Earl glanced in an obvious manner towards the window as if he were longing to be outside and she said quickly:

"Please . . . listen, then I will leave. I was on my way when a short distance from here there was a thunder-storm."

"There certainly was!" Lord Charles remarked. "I said to His Lordship we were extremely lucky that we arrived here before it broke over our heads. It upsets most horses as I imagine it upset yours."

Salrina was about to say that it did not worry Jupiter but the horse she was actually riding, then thought it immaterial.

"I took shelter, My Lord," she said, looking once again at the Earl, "in a wayside Inn. There seemed to be nobody about so I put my horse into the stables."

"Very sensible of you!" Lord Charles remarked.

"Because I saw there were people in the Inn I decided to stay in the stable," Salrina went on, "and sat down on some straw."

As she spoke the Earl stifled a yawn as if to show he was bored.

Because she knew he was making her even more nerv-ous and uncomfortable than she was already, she said quickly:

"It was then that I overheard two men in the next stall . . . plotting to . . . kill the . . . Prince Regent."

As she spoke, her words almost tumbling over themselves, she saw both gentlemen facing her stiffen and stare at her incredulously.

"Did you say they were plotting to kill the Prince Regent?" the Earl enquired.

"Yes . . . and one was a Frenchman whom I heard being paid one thousand pounds and the same amount was promised to him once His Royal Highness was . . . dead."

There was silence for a moment. Then the Earl said at last:

"Is this a joke? Who sent you here to regale us with this nonsense?"

For the first time since she had come into the house Salrina felt her nervousness leave her and instead she felt angry.

She rose from the chair saying:

"I am sorry, My Lord! I have bored you, but I thought you were the right person to approach considering it is well known that His Royal Highness honours you with his friendship. I will leave, and try to find somebody more responsible to hear what I have to say."

As she finished speaking she dropped the Earl a little curtsy and walked towards the door.

Almost immediately Lord Charles jumped up from the sofa.

"Stop!" he said. "You cannot go like this! *I* believe you, and I must hear the end of the story."

He looked at the Earl in a meaningful manner as he spoke, silently rebuking him for his behaviour.

"Really, Charles . . ." the Earl began.

But Lord Charles had moved across the room and was

standing in front of Salrina when she would have opened the door.

"Please forgive us," he said, "if we seem incredulous, but you must see that what you have just said seems almost too dramatic to be credible."

The way he spoke and the fact that it was now impossible for her to leave the room made Salrina raise her eyes to his.

"I felt the ... same," she said in a low voice, "but it is ... true!"

"I do believe you," Lord Charles said again, "so come back and tell us the rest of the story. You must realise that if this Frenchman intends to kill His Royal Highness, we must stop it."

"That is what I thought," Salrina said, "but ... I think ..."

She glanced back at the Earl, who had not moved from his armchair.

"I ... I think perhaps I had better ... go."

There was a silence. Then Lord Charles said with an edge on his voice:

"Do you want her to leave, Alaric? If she does and the Prince is assassinated, I wonder how you will feel about it."

The Earl rose from his chair.

"Please come back, Miss Milton," he said. "I apologise if I was rude, but you must be aware there have been quite a number of rumours about attempts to assassinate His Royal Highness which have never actually been made."

"I ... I did not know ... that," Salrina said almost beneath her breath.

71

Then she looked up at Lord Charles.

"I had better leave," she said piteously. "Perhaps if I ride hard I can reach the Chief Constable tonight. He lives a long way from here."

"Of course you must do nothing of the sort!" Lord Charles said. "For goodness' sake, Alaric, persuade Miss Milton that you are not indifferent to what happens to His Royal Highness. We were saying only this morning that Bonaparte is getting desperate. It is therefore quite a possibility that he would hire an assassin to dispose of the 'First Gentleman in Europe!'"

The Earl gave a short laugh that had no humour in it.

"Very well, Charles," he said. "You win! Please sit down, Miss Milton, and continue with your story."

It was more of an order than a plea, and reluctantly, feeling she hated the Earl, Salrina seated herself once again in the armchair.

"Now suppose," Lord Charles said, sitting nearer to her than he had before, "you start at the beginning and tell us exactly what happened, word for word."

In a low voice, not looking at the Earl but at Lord Charles, Salrina told him how because she was tired she had fallen asleep and had woken to hear two men speaking in low voices, one with a French accent.

Then she repeated as she could remember word for word exactly what she had heard them say and related how when the Englishman had left she had known even while she pretended to be asleep that the Frenchman was contemplating killing her.

"You really thought that?" Lord Charles asked. "It must have been extremely frightening!"

"I was . . . terrified," Salrina replied, "but somehow I managed not to move! Then the Englishman's groom arrived and they took the horses out into the yard."

"And after they had gone you left too?"

"There was no one about and I imagined the only ostler was in the Inn," Salrina said. "There was no one to pay and I just came away."

"Where were you going?" the Earl asked.

He had not spoken since she had begun to tell her tale, and she looked at him almost as if she had forgotten he was there before she replied.

"I had a message to deliver, My Lord."

"To whom?"

"I do not think that is of any importance. My only concern is that somebody in authority should know what is being planned, and I will then no longer feel it is my responsibility."

The Earl sat back in his chair.

"What you are actually saying is that Lord Charles and I must post to London to alert the Prince Regent, and of course you, Miss Milton, must be invited tomorrow night to the party which His Royal Highness is giving at Carlton House!"

There was a silence after he had spoken while Salrina stared at him in astonishment before he added:

"Very clever, if I may say so! An original way of getting yourself into the 'El Dorado' of all young women!"

"I . . . I do not know what you are . . . saying!" Salrina murmured almost beneath her breath.

"Of course you do!" the Earl said. "Is there a woman in the Kingdom who does not long to enter the 'Holy of Holies,' to be presented to 'Prince Charming' in the shape, if a somewhat portly one, of the Prince Regent, and then be able to boast to her friends of what happened?"

It took Salrina a moment to realise what he was insinuating. Then once again she rose to her feet to say in a voice that seemed to ring out round the room:

"How dare you! How dare you suggest that I would stoop to doing anything like that! I think, My Lord, you are utterly and completely despicable, and I am only sorry I was foolish enough to encroach upon your time, and what I believed was your patriotism."

So swiftly that she reached the door before Lord Charles could anticipate her, Salrina left the room and, running across the hall, she saw a footman waiting at the door.

"Do you require your horse, Madam?" he asked politely.

"I will . . . go to the stables . . . myself," Salrina replied, finding it hard to speak. "Please . . . show me the . . . way."

The footman was surprised, but he obeyed her and only as they reached the bottom of the steps and Salrina was hurrying across the gravel was she aware that Lord Charles was calling her from the front door.

"Miss Milton! Miss Milton!"

She did not turn her head, but only hurried on.

chapter four

As Salrina ran away Lord Charles turned to the Earl and said:

"Are you crazy, Alaric? What was the point of insulting the girl?"

"I do not believe one word she said!" the Earl replied abruptly.

"Well, I am convinced she is telling the truth," Lord Charles replied, "and are you prepared to risk 'Prinny's' lying dead in his blood because we, the only people who knew it might happen, did nothing to stop it?"

The Earl rose to his feet and stared at his friend for a moment before he asked:

"Can you really credit for a moment that such an absurd and ridiculous story, which might have come from some Playhouse, is actually going to happen?"

"I will take the risk if you will not!" Lord Charles answered.

For a moment the Earl hesitated, then he said:

"All right, I will apologise."

"You will have to hurry," Lord Charles said, "otherwise she will disappear and we have no idea where she lives or how we can find her again."

The Earl looked cynical as if he felt that Salrina was not likely to go far.

As he walked across the hall Lord Charles hurried ahead and started to shout her name to which Salrina paid no attention.

Having reached the entrance to the stables, which was just behind one wing of the house, she said to the first groom she saw:

"I want my horse immediately, please!"

He obviously seemed slightly surprised at seeing her in the stables, but he ran to the first of a long row of buildings which all opened onto a large, well-kept yard and Salrina followed him.

She saw that Jupiter, having had his bridle removed, was eating greedily from a manger.

He was, in fact, in the best-kept and largest stall she had ever seen, and it passed through her mind how much she wished her father could have the same accommodation for his horses.

Then as the groom started to put the bridle over Jupiter's head while he snatched a last mouthful, Salrina who was watching knew that somebody else had entered the stall.

She had expected it to be Lord Charles, but to her surprise it was the Earl, who said:

"I apologise again, Miss Milton. Forgive me for my rudeness, and please let us discuss what you overheard."

Salrina shook her head and replied for a moment:

"I have no more to say, My Lord!"

"That is not true!" the Earl contradicted. "You have not described at all clearly what the two men you saw looked like."

Salrina knew this was true.

Because he had made her nervous by what she knew was his hostile attitude, she had not gone into the details of all she had seen through the crack in the stall.

She had, in fact, felt because the Earl was so overpowering, it would seem degrading that she should have been peeping and eavesdropping on strangers.

She now wished fervently that she had not come to Fleet House but had returned to her father to let him cope with the situation.

She did not speak and after a moment the Earl said:

"Please, I do beg of you to come back to the house. I do not think this is a place where we can talk."

"There is no need for me to come back to the house, My Lord," Salrina replied. "Perhaps I could tell you what you wish to know outside in the yard."

She realised it would be a mistake to say too much in front of the groom, and she therefore moved with what she hoped was dignity past the Earl and out into the sunshine.

There she saw that Lord Charles was waiting for them and she suspected it was he who had sent the Earl after her to apologise.

She found it impossible, however, to look at either of them and instead stood a few yards from the stable door looking down at the cobblestones and praying that she could get away as quickly as possible.

Because there was silence for a moment she felt that

her attitude had somewhat disconcerted both men, and she had the idea without looking up that they exchanged glances.

Then Lord Charles said:

"If Miss Milton has forgiven you, Alaric, for your quite appalling rudeness, I suggest we discuss together over a glass of wine what can be done."

"No, no, please," Salrina cried. "I cannot stay as long as that. I have to leave!"

"I cannot believe that any appointment, Miss Milton, is more important than what you have just told us."

The Earl did not sound now as if he were sneering at her, and yet Salrina felt instinctively that he still did not believe her story.

She made a helpless little gesture with her hands.

"I have told you everything that happened," she said, "there is nothing more I can do. Surely it is quite easy for you to protect His Royal Highness now that you are aware of Napoleon Bonaparte's intention?"

She was sure as she spoke that the Earl was convinced she had fabricated the whole tale for her own ends, and nothing she could say or do would change his mind.

"I am afraid now I must go," she added.

With a feeling of relief she saw the groom approaching, leading Jupiter by his bridle out into the yard.

"I can only apologise again," the Earl said, "and beg you in all sincerity to help us prevent what would be not only a disaster to this country, but also a devastating blow to Wellington's Armies."

Salrina, who was already moving towards Jupiter, stopped.

She knew what the Earl had said was true, and that if the soldiers who were fighting desperately on foreign soil learnt of such a tragedy, it would undoubtedly lower their morale and perhaps allow the all-conquering French to be victorious once again.

She had always found it hard to think of the suffering of the men who had been so brave in the Peninsular Campaigns and who had struggled against insurmountable odds to where they were at the moment.

Because the thought of their suffering was more important than her feelings, she said in a childlike way:

"What . . . do you want me to . . . do?"

"I want you to forgive me and come back to the house and help Lord Charles and me to decide what is the best way to act in such unusual circumstances," the Earl replied.

Because it seemed foolish to go on fighting him in the yard with the groom within earshot, Salrina did not answer but turned round and walked in the direction of the house.

The Earl told the groom to take Jupiter back into the stables and Salrina found herself walking with Lord Charles on one side of her and the Earl on the other.

Nobody spoke as they climbed the steps up to the front door where the footmen were waiting.

"Bring a bottle of champagne to the Library," the Earl ordered.

"Very good, M'Lord!"

A footman hurried ahead of them to open the door into the largest and most impressive Library Salrina had ever imagined.

Books covered the walls and a balcony ran along one side, while there were long windows opening onto a flower-filled garden on the other.

It made her forget everything for the moment except

a longing to be able to sit in this room and read all the books which would tell her so much that she wished to know.

Then as the Earl indicated a sofa at the side of the fireplace she sat down on it, clasped her hands together in her lap, and raised her eyes to his.

She looked so young and so unsure of herself that unexpectedly the Earl said with a twist of his lips:

"I am very contrite! Now, let us begin again at the beginning where you came here to ask my help and to tell me something so horrifying that it is not surprising I found it difficult to believe."

Salrina drew in her breath.

She knew instinctively he was a man who found it particularly hard to apologise, and because it had always been difficult for her to bear a grudge she knew she must do what he wanted, even though she told herself she still hated him.

She hated him for his cynicism and the way in which she was certain he never considered anybody except himself.

The Earl sat down on the chair very similar to the one he had occupied in the Morning Room and Lord Charles seated himself on the sofa.

He did not sit beside Salrina but, it being a very large sofa, at the other end of it.

"Now, what I want you to do," the Earl said as if he were at a Committee Meeting, "is to tell us, Miss Milton, exactly what the Englishman looked like, and Lord Charles and I will try to identify him."

"The Frenchman mostly addressed the Englishman as 'Monsieur' but once as 'Milord,'" Salrina replied.

"That certainly narrows the field a little!" the Earl

remarked. "What age did you think he was?"

Salrina thought carefully.

"Perhaps . . . fifty, and I will try to describe him."

With great difficulty she remembered that he looked debauched, had heavy lines under his eyes, and the thickness of his chins above his starched cravat.

There was not very much except that she thought, although she did not say so, that he must be very rich, as he had given the Frenchman one thousand pounds and had promised to pay him another thousand when the Regent was dead.

"Would you recognise his voice if you heard it again?" the Earl asked.

"I . . . think so . . . I am not . . . sure."

"But you would remember his face and be able to point him out?"

Salrina did not answer.

It struck her that once again the Earl was insinuating that she was trying to inveigle an invitation to Carlton House.

As if he knew what she was thinking, Lord Charles said quickly:

"Now we have to know what the Frenchman looked like."

'He, at any rate, was easy to describe,' Salrina thought. 'A pointed nose, a "foxy" look about him, and the fact that he was dressed as smartly as any Dandy she had ever seen depicted in pictures or cartoons.'

She repeated what she had been thinking and Lord Charles exclaimed:

"Well, at least we have something to go on!"

"It will be easier of course because we will have Miss Milton with us!" the Earl said.

Salrina looked at him in consternation.

"That is something you have already suggested, My Lord," she said in a low voice, "but I want to make it very clear that there is no possible way by which I can help you any further in your search for the assassin."

"Yet it is something you absolutely must do," the Earl answered. "There is nobody but you, Miss Milton, who can recognise the Frenchman, and as there will not be many French visitors invited to Carlton House, it will be easy with your help for him to be identified by you and removed before he can do anything dangerous."

"In which case," Salrina said quickly, "it is quite obvious, My Lord, that you do not need me. Whoever is guarding His Royal Highness has only to make sure that no Frenchman is allowed to approach him during the evening, or better still, to make sure all the French are turned away when they arrive and there will be no more trouble."

She thought as she spoke she had been rather clever, but the Earl to her surprise said firmly:

"If he does not succeed tomorrow night, thanks to the precautions you have suggested, how can we be sure he will not try again?"

Salrina had not thought of that, and she told herself that although she disliked the Earl, he was certainly quick-brained.

"But after what the Englishman said," she replied somewhat lamely, "I am sure they will send the Frenchman back to France and find somebody else."

"I think that is unlikely," Lord Charles interposed. "After all, one thousand pounds is a lot of money, and the Englishman will want value for it!"

"What is more," the Earl interposed, "you have already told us that Bonaparte is also concerned in this, and the assassin will not wish to disappoint his Emperor."

"I understand what you are saying," Salrina agreed, "but there is nothing more I can do! I have to return to my father tomorrow, who is not well, and I will pray that the information I have given you will safeguard His Royal Highness's life."

"I have already said that we cannot manage without you, Miss Milton," the Earl argued.

"But you have to! Please . . . you must understand . . . you *have* to!"

There was a moment's silence, then the Earl said:

"I cannot believe that any woman who is English would not at this moment feel it her patriotic duty to support our Armies. Lord Charles and I fought in the Peninsula, and I can assure you no soldiers could have been braver than our own, and no other Army could have endured the hardship that our men suffered fighting their way through Portugal."

For the first time the Earl was speaking with a sincerity and a feeling behind his words of which Salrina was very conscious.

Now she looked at him, her large eyes studying his face, and instinctively she clasped her hands together.

"I would do anything in my power to help our soldiers," she said in a low voice. "I cannot . . . bear to think of their sufferings or the . . . casualties to both . . . men and horses!"

There was a little sob in her voice that neither the Earl nor Lord Charles missed.

After a moment Lord Charles said:

"It is because you feel like that, Miss Milton, that you must help us to strain every nerve to keep the Prince Regent alive."

"That is true," the Earl agreed. "As a soldier, I can tell you that nothing would be a greater blow, at this particular moment when we are hoping and praying that victory is not far off, than to know that the man who is a symbol of everything that is cultured and civilised should be struck down ignominiously!"

There was silence. Then Salrina asked in the same childlike way that she had before:

"W-what do you . . . want me to . . . do?"

The Earl gave what Lord Charles thought was a sigh of relief, as if he were aware they had been fighting a battle and had won.

"What I think we all ought to do," he said aloud, "is to leave as soon as possible for London. If I order my Phaeton, it will be quicker than driving any other vehicle, and we will get to my house in Berkeley Square in time for dinner!"

Salrina gave a little cry.

"I . . . I cannot do that! It is . . . quite impossible! I have to return to my father. If I am not home by morning he will be extremely . . . anxious and also very . . . angry with me."

"I am sure your father will understand the very unusual circumstances," Lord Charles said.

It flashed through Salrina's mind that her father would be utterly horrified that she should go to London with the Earl of Fleetwood and another man.

But being unable to talk to him directly, she found it impossible to find any reasonable explanation of her behaviour.

"I . . . I cannot do it!" she said. "I really . . . cannot!"

"What we must do," the Earl said, "is to send some-body to explain to your father what has happened. If you will write him a letter, I will despatch it to him imme-diately by one of my grooms. I feel sure he will under-stand."

Salrina considered this for a second or two, then she remembered that her father had told her that under no circumstances whatsoever was she to let anybody know her true identity.

Feeling as if she had suddenly stepped into a maze from which there was no way out, she wondered fran-tically what she should do.

The only idea that came into her mind was that if the Earl was ready to send a letter by a groom, it would be easier to hide her identity if she could explain everything to Mabel.

Perhaps she could find somebody who would convey the old woman to the Manor, but it all seemed rather farfetched, and perhaps Mabel would be too old and too ill to go.

Then Salrina remembered she had once or twice since she had retired visited her son at the shop, so it was not an impossibility.

"What I was going to do, My Lord," she said, choos-ing her words carefully, "was to visit somebody who lives in one of your cottages at the end of the village. If I go to see her now, I might persuade her to call on my father and explain the circumstances in which I find my-self, and she can stay the night at our house."

She thought as she spoke that it sounded such a la-borious procedure that the Earl would sweep the idea away disdainfully.

But to her relief he said:

"If that is what you wish, then of course we must agree, Miss Milton."

He looked at Lord Charles and said:

"Your suggestion that I should try to break my record has obviously been taken up by fate, for it is something I shall now attempt on the return journey!"

Lord Charles laughed.

"We have certainly had a very short visit to the country!"

Because they seemed almost to have forgotten her existence, Salrina rose.

"May I have my own horse to ride to the village?"

"Yes, of course," Lord Charles said, "I will send one of the footmen to the stables."

He walked across the room to the door, and when Salrina was alone with the Earl he said:

"I think, Miss Milton, we are very much in your debt, not only for uncovering such a ghastly plot, but also for agreeing to come with us to London."

As he spoke it swept over her exactly what that entailed, and Salrina gave a sudden cry.

"I had forgotten . . . I was not thinking . . ." she cried, "but . . . I cannot go with you to . . . Carlton House . . . how can I?"

"What do you mean?" the Earl asked.

"I have nothing to wear! How could I appear . . . dressed like . . . this?"

The Earl gave a short laugh.

"That is certainly something any other woman except yourself, Miss Milton, would have thought of first."

"It was very . . . stupid of me!" Salrina admitted, "but because I never have . . . time to worry about clothes, it never . . . struck me that I should need an . . . evening gown in which to identify an . . . assassin!"

It seemed almost amusing as she said it, and for the first time since she had been speaking to the Earl her dimples appeared on either side of her mouth.

"Well, that is not an insurmountable obstacle," he said dryly. "You will find, since we will arrive in London tonight, that you will have time tomorrow to find yourself a very suitable gown before the evening, and all the things that go with it, like gloves and slippers."

Salrina was listening, then she said in a very low voice:

"I . . . I am afraid that does not . . . solve the problem because I . . . could not afford to . . . buy them."

As she spoke she remembered the envelope that she had in her pocket containing either a cheque or notes for three hundred guineas which she had received for Orion.

But never in any circumstances however serious would she use the money that was so vitally needed not only for her father and herself, but also for their horses, on anything so frivolous as an evening gown.

"Do not worry about that," the Earl said, breaking in on her thoughts. "I will of course provide you with what you wish to wear."

The sarcastic note was back in his voice as he thought of how many women had dressed themselves at his expense and here was yet another, if very unlikely, candidate for his generosity.

Then he was aware that Salrina was staring at him before she said in a shocked voice:

"No . . . of course not! I could not possibly . . . allow you or . . . any man to . . . pay for my clothes! My mother would be . . . horrified at the idea!"

"Your mother?" the Earl asked. "Then she is at home looking after your father?"

He spoke almost as if he had caught her out, and Salrina replied:

"My mother is dead . . . but I still behave as she would expect . . . me to."

"Yes, of course," the Earl agreed, and for a moment there was a frown between his eyes.

Then he said with a note of triumph as if delighted at having solved yet another problem:

"There is no difficulty! I know at my house in London there are a number of gowns that have been left behind by my sister, who is at the moment on a visit to Ireland. She felt there she would not need the elaborate creations with which she has dazzled the *Beau Monde* in London."

Salrina thought for a moment. Then she said:

"You are quite certain your sister will not mind my borrowing . . . one of her . . . gowns?"

"My brother-in-law is serving in the Grenadier Guards," the Earl replied, "and I know my sister would gladly agree to anything if it would help her husband, who is at the moment with Wellington's Army."

Salrina smiled, then she said:

"I think I should hurry to . . . see my friend in the . . . village."

"If you tell me where you will be," the Earl said, "Lord Charles and I will pick you up in the Phaeton in about twenty minutes. That should be long enough for you to arrange everything, and if it is not, then I can come to your rescue or send a groom, as I have already suggested."

"Thank you very much," Salrina said simply.

She ran from the Library through the Hall to find, as

she expected, Lord Charles was just coming to tell her that her horse was waiting.

He went down the steps with her and lifted her into the saddle and arranged her skirt over the stirrup with an experienced hand.

Before she rode off he said:

"Promise you will not disappear like one of the goddesses, back to Olympus, and we shall never find you again."

"You will find me at Honeysuckle Cottage," Salrina replied, remembering that the Earl had forgotten to ask where she was going.

She smiled at Lord Charles, touched Jupiter with her whip, and rode off as quickly as she could.

It took her only a very short time to reach Honeysuckle Cottage, and when she arrived there, she was astonished to see there was a comfortable, closed carriage, drawn by two horses.

She wondered, as she dismounted, who could be visiting Mabel and left Jupiter free to wander onto a small patch of grass that adjoined the cottage.

She thought the two servants seated on the box of the carriage in their tall cockaded hats looked surprised, but she knew that he would not go far and would come the moment she called to him.

Opening the gate, she walked up the small path bordered by pansies to the porch, which was covered with honeysuckle, thus accounting for the name of the cottage.

She knocked and the door was opened immediately.

There stood a bright-eyed old woman looking at her in surprise.

"Miss Salrina, as I live and breathe!" she exclaimed. "I never expected to see you here today!"

Salrina bent and kissed her cheek before she said:

"It is lovely to see you, Mabel, but unfortunately I could not let you know I was coming."

As she spoke she looked across the small kitchen and saw sitting in an armchair by the stove a face she recognised.

For a moment she could hardly believe it was true.

Then as someone rose and held out their arms Salrina murmured:

"Rosemary! Is it really you?"

"I might ask the same thing!" was the reply. "And actually, I was trying to make up my mind whether to be brave enough to come and see you tomorrow."

Salrina kissed the very attractive, beautifully dressed woman, and exclaimed:

"Rosemary, I would hardly have recognised you!"

As she spoke she thought that the villagers at home too and her father would find it hard to recognise the Vicar's daughter, who had left them for the North eight years ago.

Rosemary Allen had been, Salrina's mother had always thought, a very sad case of a girl who had missed her chances of marriage through devoting herself to an ailing, querulous, and tiresome parent.

The Vicar had been a charming man, the youngest son of a Baronet who in the traditional manner had sent his oldest son into the Army, his second son into the Navy, and his third into the Church.

The Reverend Daniel Allen had unfortunately married a woman who, although of good birth, was extremely unsuitable for a Parson's wife.

She disliked the people to whom her husband preached and wanted only a social life which did not exist in the small village to which he was appointed as Vicar.

She therefore took to her bed and her daughter, their only child, became nothing more than an unpaid, unthanked Nurse.

She waited on her mother hand and foot and never had a chance to be with girls of her own age.

It was Lady Milborne who tried to bring a little happiness into Rosemary's life and to relieve her, if only for a few hours a day, from the miseries of her home.

She therefore suggested she should teach Salrina.

It had been a kind action, and as Rosemary was then eighteen and very intelligent, Salrina enjoyed her lessons and learnt a great deal from them.

The years went by, until when Rosemary was twenty-six and in the villagers' eyes at any rate a confirmed "old maid" a miracle happened.

A distant relative of her father's called to see them unexpectedly and although he was a much older man fell in love with her.

Because he wished to return to Northumberland where he lived as quickly as possible, they were married quietly in the village Church and Rosemary's only bridesmaid was Salrina.

After that she disappeared to the North and although she wrote home and sent Salrina small presents for Christmas and for her birthday, she had never until this moment seen her again.

Now it seemed impossible that she should have blossomed into anything so smart and, Salrina realised, so very attractive.

As she exclaimed over Rosemary's appearance and Rosemary repeated that she was on her way to stay with her father at the Vicarage Salrina had an idea.

"Listen, Mabel," she said, "would you think it very rude if I talked to Mrs. Whitbread alone? I have something to tell her which is a family matter."

"No, 'cors not, I understands, Miss Salrina," Mabel said. "Now, go ye into th' Parlour, an' I'll get ye both a nice cup o' tea."

"That would be lovely!" Rosemary said.

Her expensive gown rustling, she went ahead of Salrina and they found themselves in a tiny room decorated with souvenirs from Mabel's life.

There were all sorts of strange objects which Salrina knew had been given to her by the villagers and by children like herself whom she always spoiled when they came to her shop.

Rosemary sat down on a chair, saying as she did so:

"Oh, Salrina, I am so thrilled and delighted to see you! But why are you here and how could you have ridden all that way alone?"

"Now listen, Rosemary, because there is very little time," Salrina said. "I am in terrible trouble and I need your help."

"Dearest, what can have happened?" Rosemary exclaimed. "Of course I will help you in any way I can."

Quickly, because she was afraid the Earl would arrive before she had finished, Salrina told her what had occurred and Rosemary listened wide-eyed.

"Can it really be true?" she asked at the end of the story. "Oh, Salrina, how terrifying for you!"

"You do see it is imperative that I go with them? But, Rosemary, they do not know who I am, and Papa said I must use a false name, since I have ridden here alone, so I have been calling myself 'Milton.' I therefore cannot allow the Earl to do as he offered and send a groom to tell Papa that I cannot come back."

"So you want me to tell him!" Rosemary said quickly.

"Please, will you do so? And if possible stay with Papa and keep him happy? He is so miserable, and I know he would not wish to be alone tomorrow, and dine alone tonight."

"I will do anything you ask me to do," Rosemary said in her soft voice, "but, Salrina, will you be safe?"

"Of course I will!" Salrina declared. "And the moment I have identified the Frenchman, I will make the Earl send me home."

"I am not sure I ought to let you go," Rosemary said doubtfully, "but I suppose, if there are two gentlemen, you will not come to any harm. Nevertheless, I am sure your mother would not approve."

"What harm could I come to?" Salrina asked innocently.

Rosemary parted her lips to speak, then thought better of it.

Salrina was not aware that she was thinking of all she had heard about the Earl's reputation, but feeling that since he had so many women pursuing him, he was not likely to be interested in anyone as young and countrified as Salrina.

She was indeed beautiful because, as Rosemary knew, she resembled Lady Milborne, who had been one of the loveliest people she had ever seen.

At the same time, with her fair hair curling untidily over her forehead, her old and threadbare riding habit and somewhat dilapidated riding hat, it was unlikely that the fastidious Earl of Fleetwood would give her a second glance.

"You must promise me," Rosemary said in a serious

voice, "that you will come home as quickly as you can after you have identified the assailant, and if you sleep at Fleet House tonight, that you will lock your door."

"Why should I do that?"

Rosemary thought quickly and said:

"Suppose the Frenchman regrets he did not kill you when he had the chance?"

Salrina shivered.

"Of course! He might be afraid I would somehow prevent him from doing what he intends tomorrow evening. After all, I am the only person in England, except for the Englishman, who is aware what he looks like and knows what he is about to do."

"Exactly!" Rosemary agreed. "You must lock your door, Salrina, and I will tell your father that you will be back just as quickly as you can be."

"Of course I will," Salrina agreed. "After all, I will not tell the Earl who I am, but will just tell the servants to drive me back here to pick up Jupiter."

"Exactly!" Rosemary said. "I think you are being very sensible. What I have to do now is to make sure your father does not worry about you and leave you to warn Mabel that you are 'Miss Milton.'"

"That is going to be more difficult than anything else." Salrina smiled. "We know Mabel is an inveterate gossip."

"If you tell her it is vitally important that she does not give away your secret," Rosemary said, "I am sure she will, at any rate, try to keep her promise."

She rose as she spoke and kissed Salrina and said:

"I will look after you father and it will be thrilling to see him again after all these years."

"He will be astonished to see you!" Salrina replied. "How can you manage to look so smart and so pretty?"

94

Rosemary laughed.

"It can all be summed up in a few words—money! And also that I am free now to be myself for the first time in my life."

Salrina looked at her, then she said perceptively:

"I have a feeling, Rosemary, that you were not very happy in your . . . marriage."

"I do not want to talk about it," Rosemary answered in a low voice, "but what I actually did, Salrina, was to exchange one life of misery with Mama for one with my husband. He was old, disagreeable, and very, very difficult!"

"Oh, Rosemary, I am so sorry!"

"I have now been a widow for eighteen months, and what is so wonderful, Salrina, is that I am rich, very rich! Something I never expected to be in the whole of my life!"

Salrina flung her arms around Rosemary's neck and kissed her.

"Oh, Rosemary, I am so glad! If anyone deserves to be happy, it is you. You have never thought of yourself, but always of other people."

Rosemary laughed. Then she said:

"Now I am trying to be very selfish, and I am in fact ashamed that I have not been back to see Papa until now. But he always writes as if he is quite content, and I have a feeling he does not really want his well-ordered life to be disrupted."

"I think that is true," Salrina said. "So, please, Rosemary, if you can, stay with Papa at the Manor tonight, all tomorrow, and until I come back the day after."

"Perhaps your father will not want me."

Salrina laughed.

"I know he will be delighted to see you!" she said sincerely. "He was always very fond of you when you came to teach me, and Mama was so sorry because you had such a miserable life. I know she would be very happy for you now that everything is so different."

Rosemary did not reply. She merely kissed Salrina on the cheek and said:

"I must go, it would be a mistake for your Earl to find me here."

"He is not *my* Earl!" Salrina said sharply. "And if you want the truth, Rosemary, I think he is a very unpleasant, overbearing, conceited man who thinks of nobody but himself!"

"From all I have heard, that is not what other women think about him," Rosemary replied.

Then as if she were worried for Salrina she kissed her again and said:

"Promise me you will do everything I have told you, and hurry home."

Salrina nodded.

Then Rosemary was driving away and, sitting down at the kitchen table, Salrina began to impress upon Mabel how important it was to conceal her real identity from the Earl and Lord Charles.

She had just got it into Mabel's head that her father, having unwillingly allowed her to take the horse to Mr. Carstairs because he himself was incapacitated, had thought it very bad for her reputation that she should not have a groom with her, when there was the sound of wheels outside.

Looking out through the small window, she could see the Earl in his very smart Phaeton drawn by four magnificently matched horses.

"I have to go now, Mabel," she said, rising to her feet, "but promise me that you will tell anybody who should ask you, that my name is Milton."

"'Course, dearie, that's wot I'll do if they asks me," Mabel said, "an' your father's right, that he is! Ye've no right t'be gallivanting all over the countryside wi' nobody to look after ye."

"There are quite enough people outside to look after me now!" Salrina laughed.

Mabel opened the door and she went out, then, turning back on the porch, kissed the old woman again as she said:

"Take care of yourself, Mabel. I will come over one day very soon to see you again, and I am sure Papa will want to come with me."

"Ye knows I'd enjoy to see yer father," Mabel replied. "Best-lookin' man I've ever seen, and that includes 'is Lordship."

Because she said it in a low voice in case the Earl should overhear, Salrina could not help laughing and her dimples were showing as she hurried down the path to where the Phaeton was waiting for her.

Lord Charles had already stepped out of it to help her up beside the Earl.

Salrina waited a moment to pat Jupiter, who had been brought from where he had been cropping the grass, but the groom who was to ride him back to the Earl's stables.

"Be a good boy," she admonished Jupiter, "and I know you will enjoy being in such luxurious surroundings."

The groom grinned.

"'E'll be orl roight, Ma'am."

"I am sure he will," Salrina replied.

She went back to the Phaeton, where Lord Charles

helped her up into it, and she realised she was to sit between him and the Earl.

It was a position to which she felt somewhat squeezed, as the Phaeton was really made to seat two persons and no more.

"Are you feeling worried that your horse will not be properly looked after in your absence?" the Earl asked.

Salrina was not quite certain if he was speaking seriously or teasing her, so she replied:

"Your stables are far more luxurious than anything he is used to. At the same time, because he belongs to me and is therefore very special, I would not like him to think I had deserted him."

They drove off, Mabel waving from the doorway and Salrina waving back.

"How is it that you know someone who lives in one of my cottages?" the Earl asked.

"I expect you are aware that Mrs. Green kept a shop before she retired, when her son, who used to work for Your Lordship, decided to take it over," Salrina replied.

"That is something I did not know," the Earl answered dryly, "any more than I was aware that the person in that rather pretty little cottage was called 'Green.'"

Salrina looked at him in surprise.

"I should have thought," she said, "you would have known the names of most of your tenants, especially those who are so near to your house."

"I suppose my mother knew them all," the Earl said, "but I must excuse myself by saying that, having been abroad for several years, many of them have died or as in the case of your friend, are new to the estate."

He spoke defensively and Salrina had the feeling that he thought she was accusing him of not being interested enough in what were his own people.

She thought that was actually what she would like to do, because he had never asked her father or anyone living locally to his Steeplechases.

There was no reason why he should do so, but she was sure that if her father had been in the same position, he and her mother would have known everybody in the community, rich or poor, and made them feel they would always help them if they could.

She was rather startled when the Earl said:

"I have a feeling, Miss Milton, that you are criticising me!"

She had no idea he could be so perceptive, and she turned her head to look at him, her eyes very large and surprised in her small face.

Then she said a little uncomfortably:

"I cannot think why Your Lordship should think that!"

"Nor can I, as it happens," the Earl remarked, "and I find it very strange!"

chapter five

THEY had driven for some time when the Earl said:

"I think we will have to concoct a good story as to why Miss Milton is arriving in London with no luggage."

As he spoke Salrina gave a start as she remembered that in her hurry to leave Mabel's cottage she had forgotten that the things she had taken with her for the night were still strapped to Jupiter's saddle.

She was just about to explain how careless she had been when she thought there was no point in muddling the issue, for the one nightgown and hairbrush she had brought with her would not be very helpful when she needed so many other things.

"I see your point," Lord Charles said in reply to the Earl, "and as your sister is away it might be an idea to say that Miss Milton is a friend of hers whom you invited to stay at your sister's request, who had lost her luggage on the way."

The Earl laughed.

"Charles, you are a genius! It sounds a very plausible story, and one that will convince the servants at Berkeley Square that there is nothing strange in Miss Milton arriving with us."

Salrina said nothing, thinking it best for them to work it out between them.

When they arrived in London, having taken, in fact, five minutes more than the Earl's last record, she was glad she had not interfered.

When they reached Berkeley Square, since a groom had ridden ahead of them to announce the Earl's arrival, the red carpet was ready to be rolled over the pavement outside and the Butler and footmen were waiting in the hall.

"Good evening, M'Lord!" Bateson said respectfully. "I hope Your Lordship had a good journey."

"Passable!" the Earl replied. "I wish to speak to Mrs. Freeman."

"Certainly, M'Lord. Champagne and pâté sandwiches are in the Library, or perhaps the young lady would prefer tea?"

Before the Earl could reply Salrina said eagerly:

"I would love a cup of tea!"

"Tea then, Bateson!" the Earl ordered as the footmen hurried ahead of them to open the door into the Library.

It was a very attractive room, by no means as large as the Library at Fleet, yet looking round the walls Salrina knew it would be a joy beyond words to be able to browse amongst the books.

The door opened, but it was Mr. Stevenson who came into the room.

"I am glad you are back, My Lord," he said in a worried tone. "I have in fact despatched a groom to you this morning to remind you that His Royal Highness is expecting you and His Lordship to dinner tomorrow night, and a message has come to say even if you were in the country, he still desires your presence."

The Earl looked at Lord Charles and laughed.

"We must have been clairvoyant, Charles, in being aware that 'Prinny' could not do without us!"

"Of course!" Lord Charles answered.

"Send a message to His Royal Highness," the Earl said to his secretary, "that Lord Charles and I have returned and are looking forward to tomorrow night. Also inform him that I will call to pay my respects tomorrow morning."

Mr. Stevenson left the room and Lord Charles said:

"Are you going to tell him that you suspect he may be murdered in cold blood?"

"No, of course not," the Earl said sharply. "He would be in a terrible tizzy and doubtless call the party off, which would mean the assassin will try again another time. No, I shall make myself pleasant, ask permission to bring Miss Milton with us as an extra guest, and, of course, see General What's-his-name, who is supposed to be in charge of security."

"I would not trust him not to make a mess of it," Lord Charles answered.

"Nor would I," the Earl agreed, "so we had better make our own plans, you and I, including making sure that one or two of the more trustworthy *Aides-de-Camp* are in on the secret."

"As there is nothing you enjoy more than organising us poor mortals," Lord Charles remarked mockingly, "I will leave everything in your capable hands!"

"Quite right!" the Earl agreed.

The door opened once again and this time it was an elderly woman wearing rustling black silk with a silver chatelaine hanging from her waist which proclaimed her to be the Housekeeper.

She dropped the Earl a curtsy, saying:

"I understands Your Lordship wishes to see me."

"I do indeed, Mrs. Freeman," the Earl replied. "Lord Charles and I have brought from the country a friend of Her Ladyship's who has arrived from Ireland so as to attend His Royal Highness's party at Carlton House tomorrow night."

Mrs. Freeman made a little bob in Salrina's direction as the Earl went on.

"Unfortunately, although it might be expected as she travelled on an Irish ship, her luggage has been lost on the voyage, and she has literally nothing to wear but what she stands up in!"

"Goodness gracious me!" Mrs. Freeman exclaimed. "What a catastrophe!"

"As there is no time for Miss Milton to buy anything for herself, especially a gown suitable for tomorrow evening," the Earl continued, "she must, of course, borrow one of those Her Ladyship has left behind. I am quite sure there are plenty to choose from."

Mrs. Freeman smiled.

"There is indeed, M'Lord! In fact I was only thinking after Her Ladyship left I'd no idea where I was going to put so many gowns. If Your Lordship has many guests to stay, we'll be hard pressed to find room for them!"

"There is only this one guest at the moment, Mrs. Freeman," the Earl said, "and I want you to look after her and find her everything she requires until her luggage arrives."

"I will do that, M'Lord!" Mrs. Freeman replied. "Perhaps the young lady'd like to come upstairs with me now to tidy herself before tea? I know how fast Your Lordship drives in those newfangled carriages with their oversize wheels!"

There was a slight note of disapproval in Mrs. Freeman's voice, but the Earl only laughed.

"Off you go, Miss Milton," he said. "Mrs. Freeman will look after you, and the tea will be here by the time you get back."

Because she knew that her hair had been blown about by the speed at which they had driven and also felt that her habit looked older and more threadbare than usual in such luxurious surroundings, Salrina was only too eager to change, if it was possible, into a gown that had belonged to the Earl's sister.

She had already learnt from Lord Charles, who had thought it important for her to know a little about her supposed friend, that the Earl's sister was Lady Caroline Forsythe.

Her husband was a soldier in the Grenadier Guards, and was already a Colonel although he was only a year or so older than his brother-in-law.

"What age is Lady Caroline?" Salrina had asked, feeling it was the sort of thing she should know.

"Twenty-seven or twenty-eight," Lord Charles replied vaguely, "and she is very attractive, although one would not strictly call her beautiful."

Salrina thought that, difficult and disagreeable though

he might be, the Earl was the most handsome man she had ever seen and it would be impossible for one of his family not to be good-looking.

But she had listened to what Lord Charles was telling her and made no comment.

Now when Mrs. Freeman showed her into a very beautiful bedroom with windows overlooking Berkeley Square she pulled off her hat and in the mirror saw with dismay how wild her hair was.

"I look a mess!" she said, speaking aloud.

"Don't worry, Miss," Mrs. Freeman said. "Her Ladyship has an excellent hairdresser who'll come to you tomorrow morning and of course again tomorrow evening. What I suggest now, if you'll excuse the presumption, is that you undress and rest for a few minutes while we prepare your bath, then it'll soon be time for dinner, and I'll find you something pretty and comfortable for this evening. Tomorrow any alterations that are necessary to your evening gown can be arranged."

Salrina thought this was an excellent idea, but she said:

"His Lordship has ordered tea for me downstairs."

"I'll send a message that you'd like it brought up here," Mrs. Freeman replied.

As she spoke she put out her hand towards the bell pull that hung from the ceiling near the canopied bed.

*   *   *

When Salrina awoke the next morning, she felt as she opened her eyes that she must still be dreaming.

She had quite expected to find that everything that

106

had happened the previous day had been an illusion.

But by the light coming in from the sides of the brocade curtains she could see the outline of the carved and gilt mirror on the dressing table and the soft lace cushions on a *chaise longue* on which she had rested before her bath.

Two housemaids in starched white caps and aprons had carried in a round bath which they stood in front of the fireplace.

Then there were cans of hot and cold water to which was added the scent of verbena, and a Turkish towel with which to dry herself which was so soft that she felt she might have been enveloped in a cloud.

It was all so different from the way she had to bathe at home that it was a delight in itself.

She knew the Earl would accept it as a matter of course and never realise what it meant to somebody who had never previously enjoyed such luxury.

After she had bathed Mrs. Freeman brought underclothes that she had never imagined existed.

There were few of them because, as Mrs. Freeman explained, gowns were straight and it was the ambition of every fashionable lady to look as slim and insubstantial as a nymph.

"I thinks Her Ladyship were slim," Mrs. Freeman said, "but I can quite see, Miss, that her dresses'll have to be taken in for you."

Salrina looked concerned.

"Perhaps Her Ladyship would object to her gowns being altered, however skilfully it is done."

"I'm sure Her Ladyship'll be only too delighted for you to borrow anything you want, Miss, and I'll be very surprised if when Her Ladyship returns she doesn't want any of what is here, but'll go out and buy herself a whole new wardrobe."

Reassured by this, Salrina made no further objections when Mrs. Freeman called in a woman who she was told was the house seamstress.

She was instructed that any gown Salrina wore tomorrow, either in the day or in the evening, would have to be taken in one and a half inches round the waist, and more on the bust.

Mrs. Freeman then produced a very pretty gown of pale blue gauze that matched Salrina's eyes and which she informed her Lady Caroline had bought by mistake and had always thought it too young to be of any use.

"In fact, I don't mind telling you, Miss, Her Ladyship wore it only once. Terrible she is over her clothes! But then she's known for being very smart, and as I always says: 'You can't make an omelette without breaking eggs!'"

Salrina laughed.

After one of the housemaids had arranged her hair in what she was told was the latest fashion and added two white roses to the curls on each side of her face, she thought it would be hard even for her father to recognise her.

"Thank you, thank you very much!" she said to Mrs. Freeman.

Then, afraid she might be late for dinner and annoy the Earl, she hurried down the stairs and into the Library, where they were to meet.

If the Earl had seemed elegant in his driving clothes,

he looked very smart indeed dressed for dinner, and so did Lord Charles.

Because tonight they were informal he did not wear knee-breeches, but the new long black drainpipe trousers that had been invented by the Prince Regent.

They both watched Salrina coming towards them and when she dropped the Earl a little curtsy he said:

"I am glad to see my sister's wardrobe has been of use!"

"I am very grateful," Salrina replied, "and very, very excited! I have never worn such a wonderful gown before and, for that matter, I have never slept in such a beautiful bedroom."

The Earl smiled.

"I expect if you stayed longer you would find fault with it, and undoubtedly grow bored."

"I should do nothing of the sort!" Salrina replied. "Papa has always said that if people are bored, it is because they do not use their brains!"

She saw Lord Charles's eyes twinkle as he looked at the Earl and heard him say quietly:

"'Out of the mouths of babes and sucklings,' Alaric!"

"Your father must be a very fortunate man," the Earl remarked, "if he finds life always amusing. What does he do?"

Salrina thought quickly what she should reply, knowing she must not reveal anything of importance, and she merely said evasively:

"Papa loves the country, and I think if I am honest it is not where one is that can be boring, but perhaps . . . just people."

"There you are, Alaric!" Lord Charles teased. "I have

109

always said it is the sort of people with whom we associate that make you yawn."

"Shut up, Charles!" the Earl said. "I will not have you lecture me!"

"It is only what you were saying yourself," Lord Charles argued. "You were reminding me yesterday morning that we were never bored in Portugal."

"Were you fighting on the Peninsula?" Salrina asked. "It must have been very uncomfortable and very frightening. I am sure that was certainly a place where one could not possibly be bored."

"You are right," Lord Charles agreed, "and that is exactly what His Lordship and I were saying yesterday when he was telling me that he was bored with London. And now, if you were a witch, you have magicked his boredom away from him!"

Salrina looked uncomfortably at the Earl and he said:

"Actually it is true! There is certainly no time to be bored at the moment, and we all have to use our brains to make quite certain that the French do not score a victory that would reverberate throughout the whole of Europe."

He spoke quite seriously, and now for the first time Salrina thought he really believed her story and no longer suspected she was making excuses in order to get herself invited to Carlton House.

She was still shocked and affronted that he should have imagined for one moment she could do such a thing.

Then she supposed that if she was a Society Débutante, which she had never been, it would be very exciting to see the inside of the house that had been written about and talked about for years, usually critically because of the amount of money that it had cost.

Almost as if the Earl were reading her thoughts he said:

"Yes, you will be coming to Carlton House tomorrow night, but I do not think, because you are a very sensible person, that you will feel nervous and certainly not bored!"

"I shall be very frightened of making mistakes," Salrina said quietly. "Suppose I point out the wrong man and when you arrest him he is innocent?"

No one spoke and she went on.

"Or worse still, I fail to recognise the Frenchman?"

Even as she spoke she knew that would be impossible.

She felt as if everything about him was imprinted on her memory, and if she shut her eyes she could still see his face quite clearly as she had seen it through the crack in the wood.

"Do not worry tonight, at any rate," the Earl said kindly. "Dinner should be ready by now."

He looked at the clock on the mantelpiece.

At that moment Bateson opened the door to say:

"Dinner is served, M'Lord!"

"On the stroke!" Lord Charles added. "Your house is perfection, Alaric, and there is no use trying to find fault with it."

The Earl did not reply; he only offered Salrina his arm and she was glad she remembered her mother had told her that was how ladies and gentlemen in grand houses processed into dinner.

At home her mother did most of the cooking because she wanted to make dishes her father enjoyed and when they were ready she would say to Salrina:

"Fetch Papa quickly! The soufflé will be exactly right in two minutes, and I could not bear it to fall flat!"

Then Salrina would run down the passage to find her

father, and pulling him by the hand would hurry him into the Dining Room.

Looking back, their meals, however scanty, had always been a time for laughter.

It was only after her mother died that her father would sit at the end of the table playing about with his food and saying he was not hungry, however hard Nanny and Salrina would try to tempt him with dishes he liked.

Sitting in the elegant Dining Room with its polished table uncovered by a tablecloth, a fashion which Salrina learnt had been brought in by the Prince Regent, she knew dinner was going to be something very different from any meal she had ever eaten before.

Thinking of it now, she knew it was not only because the food was delicious and she was offered several dishes she had never heard of, but also because she was listening to two handsome, attractive men duelling with each other in words and capping each other's jokes.

Lord Charles frequently teased the Earl, who always had a quick *repartée,* which made Salrina aware, as she had thought already, that he was very quick-brained.

'Perhaps the reason why he is bored is that most of the people he meets are not as intelligent as he is,' she told herself.

She remembered her mother had always said:

"A man will be attracted by a pretty face, my dearest, but to love a woman he wants much more than good looks."

"What do you mean, Mama?" Salrina had asked when she was quite young.

Her mother had looked serious as she said:

"To make a man happy a woman has to be loving, compassionate, and very sympathetic. But she also has to stimulate his mind and keep him alert and interested. Most of all she has to inspire him to do the best of which he is capable and to try to reach the stars."

Her mother had given a little sigh before she added:

"Sometimes the stars are out of reach, but both men and women still go on trying to touch them."

Salrina at the time had puzzled over what her mother had meant, but later when she read the books her mother wished her to read and studied the subjects her mother thought would interest and inspire her, she began to understand.

She would hear her father and mother discussing world affairs and the customs of other countries that had nothing whatsoever to do with their everyday life.

And she knew that in that way her mother kept her father's mind interested in things which were outside their immediate sphere yet still remained a part of his life, even though he was too poor to travel.

* * *

"You are very quiet, Miss Milton," the Earl said at the end of dinner when he and Lord Charles had been talking animatedly to each other.

"I am listening," Salrina replied, "and I do not believe any drama in a Playhouse could be more exciting or indeed more brilliant!"

The Earl looked at her for a moment. Then he said:

"I think, Charles, that is the most ingenuous and flattering compliment you or I will ever receive!"

Salrina blushed.

"I was not trying to flatter you, My Lord. It was just that you were talking in a way I always expected intelligent men to talk, but thought I would never have the opportunity of hearing it."

"That is interesting," the Earl said, "and tell me, Miss Milton, why should you have thought intelligent men would talk in such a way?"

Salrina smiled before she replied.

"I have read the Restoration Comedies, My Lord."

"Of course!" the Earl said. "Now, Charlie, you must be aware of the standard we have to live up to in future."

"I think you have been rather remiss in not letting Miss Milton play a part in these Cheltenham Dramatics," Lord Charles said.

Salrina gave a little cry.

"No, please . . . I am very happy to be the audience. I remember Mama, when she told me how to give a successful party, always said if one has a celebrity, or two or three of them, one must be always certain they will have enough admirers to make them feel they are the centre of attention."

Both the men laughed, then dinner was over and they all moved, although Salrina suggested she should leave them with their port, back into the Library.

"I have a feeling, Miss Milton," the Earl said, "that you are admiring my books."

"I was thinking, My Lord," Salrina replied, "that it would be like walking into Heaven to be able to sit down and read them all or, better still, start with the Library you have in the country."

She did not see the amused smile on the Earl's face at the way she spoke because she was staring round the room, trying to read the titles on the books, and wondering if she ever had the chance to do so, which one she would read first.

All too quickly, it seemed to her, the evening was

over and the Earl said that because they had had a long day, with so much to do tomorrow, and undoubtedly it would be a nerve-racking evening, they should go to bed early.

Only as Salrina went up the stairs having said good night after Lord Charles had escorted her into the hall did she wonder if perhaps the two gentlemen were going out to enjoy themselves after what must for them have been a rather dull evening alone with her.

It was a lowering thought, at the same time she did not linger on it because there was so much else to think about.

After the maid had undone her gown and she had got into the large, comfortable bed with lace-edged sheets and pillowcases, both embroidered with the Earl's monogram, she fell asleep almost before she could say her prayers.

Now she thought that, whatever happened in the future, she would have so many marvellous things to remember that she would never again regret that she could not attend the Balls and parties which her mother had described to her.

'Meeting the Prince Regent will be the same as being presented at Buckingham Palace!' she thought, and told herself she was the luckiest girl in the world.

* * *

She rang the bell and was astonished to find it was after nine o'clock.

"I must get up!" she exclaimed.

"Oh, no, Miss," Mrs. Freeman replied, who had come into the room after the maids had drawn the curtains.

"I've brought you breakfast in bed, and His Lordship says you're to rest for as long as possible. He'll not be back until luncheon time."

"His Lordship has gone out?"

"Yes, Miss, His Lordship's gone riding."

Salrina wished she could have gone riding with him, then told herself she could hardly ride in Rotten Row dressed in her old habit.

In fact, if she had accompanied the Earl, he would certainly have been ashamed of her.

'He is so very smart,' she told herself, 'and I expect he has a lovely lady, or perhaps several of them, wanting to ride with him.'

She remembered all she had heard said about him in the country, about his parties and the reputation he had for being pursued by dozens of beautiful women who wanted to marry him.

Of course by the time the tales reached that isolated part of the country in which their Manor House was situated, Salrina was certain they had been distorted and perhaps had no foundation at all in fact.

But having seen him, she thought the tales of his many love affairs were probably not exaggerated but merely to be expected.

She thought in the future she would be more attentive to everything that was said about him, because she had actually been with him in an adventure which, if they ever heard about it, nobody would believe.

When she had finished her breakfast, Mrs. Freeman had come back to talk about her clothes for the evening.

She was shown several gowns that she might wear that night at Carlton House and was informed that the one she chose would be altered to fit her.

They were all so lovely that Salrina stared at them in astonishment.

The Earl had said that his sister had not taken her most glamorous gowns with her to Ireland, and it was not surprising.

The fashion had altered since the beginning of the century, when straight gowns with high waists had first come in.

But now the hems and bodices of dresses were very elaborate, even though the gowns themselves were still straight and high-waisted.

Lady Caroline's gowns, perhaps because she was older and very fashion-conscious, were, Salrina thought, a riot of lace, embroidery, frills, and bunches of flowers.

At first she was a little bewildered by what Mrs. Freeman showed her.

Then she tried to think what her mother would choose for her if she knew she was going to such an important party.

There was one gown which Salrina was sure would have been her mother's choice.

It was white and rather less elaborate than the others, but the white gauze had a slip under it of silver, and silver ribbons crossing over the breast.

The hem was decorated with white camelias that had silver leaves.

"That one is lovely!" she exclaimed. "May I wear that, unless Lady Caroline is keeping it for something special?"

"Now, it's strange you should say that, Miss," Mrs. Freeman said, "because Her Ladyship always disliked that gown after she had bought it. Twice she's put it on to go to a Ball only to take it off again!"

"'It does not suit me!' she says, and changes into something else!"

"But it is the one I would like to wear," Salrina insisted.

"Then I'm sure you're very welcome, Miss," Mrs. Freeman said, "and I'm quite sure it'll suit you."

It was taken away to be altered, and when Salrina was dressed in a very elegant day gown of pale green muslin like the leaves of Spring, Mrs. Freeman produced a very pretty high-crowned bonnet trimmed with small yellow flowers to go with it.

Because she felt so different and almost as if she were in fancy dress, Salrina went downstairs carrying her bonnet in her hand to put it on after luncheon.

She felt it would be a crime to spoil the elegance of her hair that had been coiffured for the first time in her life by a professional hairdresser.

When it was finished she hardly recognised herself.

Her curly hair, instead of running riot, now framed her small face. At the same time, it accentuated the oval sweep of her forehead, which she had never noticed before, and the point of her small chin.

"You looks lovely, Miss, and that's the truth!" Mrs. Freeman said. "I'm sure His Lordship'll think so too."

Salrina wanted to say that it was very doubtful that His Lordship would take any notice.

But as she went into the Library where the Earl and Lord Charles were having a glass of champagne before luncheon, she saw his eyes flicker over her.

Although he said nothing, she thought he not only approved of her appearance but was also surprised that she could look so unlike the girl he had brought to London.

Lord Charles however was not so reticent.

"There is no need to tell you, Miss Milton, how lovely you look!" he said. "I am sure your mirror has done that for you."

"I thought there must be something wrong with the glass!" Salrina replied. "And I remembered how my Nanny always said: 'Fine feathers make fine birds, and it's your character that counts, not your face!'"

Both men laughed.

"I can remember my Nanny saying very much the same thing," Lord Charles said. "I am sure your Nanny did too, Alaric?"

"My Nanny always said: 'I'll make you into a gentleman if I have to beat the devil out of you!'" the Earl replied. "And she did!"

They were still laughing when luncheon was announced and once again it was a meal at which were said so many things too brilliant to be forgotten that Salrina wished she could write them down quickly so as to preserve them for all time.

When they had finished, the Earl asked Salrina what she would like to do.

"Do you really mean I can choose?" she asked.

"Within reason," the Earl replied cautiously.

"Then could we possibly go to Tattersall's?"

"Tattersall's?" the Earl exclaimed.

"Perhaps it would be impossible," Salrina said, "but I have always heard that the best horses are sold there and it would be wonderful for me to see them."

As she spoke she remembered how often her father had said:

"If only I could afford to go to Tattersall's and buy a really well-bred stallion and a few fine mares, I know, although it would take time, I could make a fortune!"

"Well, of course we can go to Tattersall's," Lord Charles said. "I happen to know there is a sale on tomorrow, and the horses will be on view today, so there is no reason why Miss Milton should not see them."

"I have no wish to go if it would bore you," Salrina said anxiously.

"As a matter of fact, it is something I want to do anyway," the Earl answered, "because I have just remembered who will be putting his stable up for sale."

He looked at Lord Charles as he spoke, who said:

"That is another thing you forgot when we posted off to the country in that precipitate manner."

"It was obviously fate that I should do so," the Earl agreed. "Do not forget, if we had not been in the country, Miss Milton would not have come to ask for our help, and anybody else she had gone to would not have been efficient as we shall be, in saving 'Prinny'!"

Salrina gave a little cry.

"Touch wood! Please touch wood! You are boasting, and it is always unlucky!"

The Earl looked surprised, but he touched the polished table with his fingers, and said:

"You have accused me of quite a number of things since we have known each other, Miss Milton, and now we must add boasting to the list!"

She looked at him a little shyly to see if he was angry. Then she laughed.

"I think, My Lord, you must be excused because you have indeed so much to boast about."

"My possessions?" he asked.

"Those you inherited, but Mrs. Freeman told me that you won a medal for gallantry when you were in the

Army, and that is more important than anything else."

For a moment there was silence, as if the Earl were astonished by what Salrina had said.

Then as he felt slightly embarrassed he rose, saying:

"If we are to go to Tattersall's we must go at once, otherwise there may be such a crowd that we cannot get near to the horses we want to see."

They drove three in the Earl's Phaeton as they had done on their way to London, and the next two hours were a delight to Salrina it was hard to express.

She only kept wishing her father were with her, for she knew he would find the horses so exciting and certainly very different in every way from the untrained wild creatures he bought, on the selling of which, after training them, he made a living.

Salrina had not forgotten the very precious package she had received for Orion, and when she undressed she had put it into a drawer of the dressing table.

As she did so she had realised that it was too fat to be a cheque, and as the farmers preferred to deal in notes, since the majority of them did not trust Banks, this was what she might have expected.

She wondered as she walked round the stalls, the Earl and Lord Charles arguing over the horses and pointing out each animal's defects, whether if she saw an exceptional bargain she should buy it on her father's behalf.

Then she realised that anything she saw in Tattersall's would fetch far too high a price and what was more, the first things that had to be paid for with the three hundred guineas were their debts.

Above all, they must purchase more food for the animals they already had in training.

Without meaning to, she showed herself to be so

knowledgeable about the animals they inspected that the Earl raised his eyebrows, although she was not aware of it, and Lord Charles listened in surprise.

As they drove home she said with a sigh of pleasure:

"Thank you very, very much! Now I have seen Tattersall's, the most famous SaleRooms for horses in the world, and I can understand why customers often spend more than they can afford there."

"What do you know about it?" the Earl asked.

"My father has a friend who told him he had bankrupted himself buying hunters that cost far more than he should have spent. Funnily enough, when he sold them again they had doubled in value in the six months during which he had owned them!"

"That is certainly a success story which Tattersall's would enjoy!" Lord Charles exclaimed.

"Nevertheless, a risky way to gamble," the Earl said dryly.

They drove back to Berkeley Square and the Earl insisted that Salrina should go to lie down before the evening.

"You must look your best and feel your best," he explained, "and be on the alert from the very first moment we step into Carlton House."

"I know I must do that," Salrina said in a low voice, "and I am . . . praying very, very hard that I shall not . . . fail you."

The Earl looked at her as if he questioned whether or not that was true.

Then as his eyes met hers Salrina found it hard to look away.

When she was alone in her bedroom with the curtains drawn, being told by Mrs. Freeman she was to sleep for nearly an hour before she need get up, she found herself thinking about the Earl.

'He is a very strange man!' she thought. 'I do not hate him anymore, but he frightens me, and I think he wastes his brain instead of doing something active and worthwhile to help England.'

She was not quite certain what he should do, but was sure that all she had heard about him in the past indicated a waste of someone who was so intelligent.

Then she told herself it would seem very impertinent of her if he knew what she was thinking, and anyway it was none of her business.

"After tomorrow I shall never see him again," she said, "but it will be difficult to forget him."

It was her last thought before she fell asleep to awake with a start when the maids came into the room to draw back the curtains and bring in her bath.

The water was scented with the fragrance of carnations and she learned that the perfumes came from a shop in Jermyn Street called Floris, which was patronised by the Prince Regent.

"I have never smelt anything so lovely!" Salrina said to Mrs. Freeman.

"I'll give you a bottle when you leave, Miss," the Housekeeper replied. "You must tell me which fragrance you prefer so that when it's finished you can order some more for yourself."

Salrina longed to say that was an extravagance that would never happen.

Instead she thanked Mrs. Freeman and said for the moment, at any rate, she preferred carnation to verbena.

"Tomorrow, Miss, you shall try gardenia," Mrs. Freeman promised.

Salrina reckoned that would be the last bath she would ever take as the Earl's guest.

When she was dressed she could hardly believe that she was not a Princess who had stepped out of a Fairy Tale.

The white gown which had really been too young for Lady Caroline looked exactly right on Salrina.

There were camelias with silver leaves to wear at the back of her head, and Mrs. Freeman must have spoken to the Earl, for when she was dressed Mr. Stevenson knocked on her door and offered her a necklace to wear of perfect pearls which were resting in a velvet-lined jewel box.

"His Lordship's compliments, Miss!" Mr. Stevenson said. "He asked me to bring you these from the safe."

"Pearls!" Salrina exclaimed. "But . . . I cannot wear those! Suppose I . . . lost them?"

"There is a safety clasp which Mrs. Freeman will fasten for you," Mr. Stevenson said. "They belonged to His Lordship's mother when she was a girl, and nobody has worn them for a very long time."

He smiled at the surprise on Salrina's face and added:

"Actually, Miss Milton, if you wear them tonight you will be doing the family a real kindness."

"What do you mean?" Salrina asked.

"Pearls only live if they are worn regularly next to the skin," Mr. Stevenson replied. "I mentioned this to Lady Caroline only a short time ago and suggested she should wear them, since otherwise they would change colour."

"What did she reply?" Salrina asked.

"She said they were too young for her and she pre-ferred diamonds," Mr. Stevenson smiled. "So you do see, Miss Milton, that you will do us a good turn if you wear them tonight."

"You are making it very easy for me to say yes, Mr. Stevenson," Salrina answered, "and actually I am longing to wear something so beautiful. I suppose I shall never have any pearls of my own, but I shall always remember these."

"Now, don't you go saying things like that, Miss!" Mrs. Freeman interposed. "I'm sure looking as lovely as you do now there will be a dozen young gentlemen asking you to marry them. And you must be very careful to choose one who can afford to give you a pearl necklace, and much more besides!"

Salrina laughed, but thought it was very unlikely.

When she went downstairs to where the Earl and Lord Charles were waiting for her she thought she would tell them how pleased she was with her pearls.

Then as she entered the Library she looked at them and gasped.

If they had seemed smart last night dressed in their evening clothes, tonight in the full regalia of silk stockings and knee breeches, and with decorations on their evening coats, they were stupendous.

The Earl wore a cross on a ribbon round his neck, which Salrina guessed was the decoration for gallantry, and Lord Charles was also wearing medals.

As she joined them she knew without being told that they approved of her appearance and Lord Charles put it into words by saying:

"You look as if you have just emerged from the lake at Fleet, or else floated down from a Planet to bemuse and bewitch us human beings!"

"Very poetic, Charles!" the Earl said. "At the same

time, Miss Milton, I must congratulate you as I know everybody will congratulate me tonight on having with me anybody so beautiful in our cynical and bored *Beau Ton!*"

Salrina laughed at the word bored, knowing it had a special meaning for them all.

Then she agreed just to sip the champagne they gave her before they drove off in the Earl's large and comfortable carriage that was waiting for them outside.

His coat-of-arms was emblazoned on the doors and the horses' harness was a burnished silver.

"I am sure," Salrina said as they drove off, "this is an illusion! I shall wake up to find myself at home, while your carriage is nothing but a pumpkin!"

The Earl laughed.

"As your Fairy Godfather, I can promise you, you are going to the Ball, although you will find when you get there that 'Prince Charming' is rather overaged and portly!"

"At the same time, very, very precious!" Salrina said.

"Of course!" the Earl agreed. "And now we must talk seriously for a moment. When you see the man we are looking for, you must not draw my attention or Charles's in a way that might warn him. Instead I suggest that you carry your handkerchief in your hand, and when you are quite certain the assailant is present, you drop it."

"Supposing before I can do so . . . he manages to . . . shoot His Royal Highness?" Salrina asked in a frightened voice.

"Charles and I have been discussing it, and we are quite certain he will not do that."

"Why not?" Salrina enquired.

"Because before he could draw out a pistol from his

pocket, a very difficult thing anyway to conceal in these clothes, he would be seen and we would seize him."

"Then what do you think he will do?" Salrina enquired.

"We are both convinced that he will use a dagger, or rather what the Italians call a stiletto. The French carried them in night attacks on our troops when they did not wish to raise the alarm!"

"That's right," Lord Charles murmured.

"They would creep up to where men were sleeping in tents or in the open," the Earl continued. "A soldier would be stabbed in the heart or the throat before he could even open his eyes and long before he could give the alarm to anyone near him."

"I see what you mean," Salrina said reflectingly.

"What I think," the Earl went on, "is that the assassin will strike when he is presented to His Royal Highness. He will offer the present from the *Marquis* you heard mentioned, and as the Regent takes it, he will stab him quickly and skilfully either in the heart or in the space between the ribs where a man can be killed instantly."

Salrina gave a little cry of horror and the Earl added:

"A dagger can be so sharp and thin that if he is as skilful as we think he must be, he will have time to move away before the Prince actually falls down to the ground. In those few seconds, while everybody's attention is centred on the man who is dying, the assailant escapes."

Salrina clapped her hands together.

"You frighten me!" she said in a low voice. "And if it is so quick . . . we might be too . . . late."

The fear in her voice was very obvious and the Earl reached out his hand to lay it over hers.

"We will not be too late," he said, "but it all depends

on you, Miss Milton! I think it was a very lucky day for
His Royal Highness when you overheard quite by chance
this dastardly plot being planned."

Without meaning to, Salrina's fingers tightened on
his.

"You are . . . quite sure I will not . . . fail you?"

"Quite, quite sure," the Earl said very quietly.

chapter six

CARLTON House was all that Salrina had expected it to be.

The splendid hall decorated with Ionic columns of brown Sienna marble was very impressive.

As they went up the graceful double staircase she wished she was not so agitated about what might happen and could really enjoy what she was seeing.

Beyond the Music Room into which they were led first, there was a Drawing Room decorated in the Chinese taste about which Salrina had read many criticisms in the newspapers.

When it had first been finished she remembered her mother saying to her father:

"It seems incredible that the mercer's bill to visit China and buy the furniture for just one room amounted to six thousand eight hundred seventeen pounds!"

"I agree it seems incredible," her father replied. "I would rather have spent such a sum on horses!"

They both laughed, but Salrina remembered over the years there had been the same sort of complaints over clocks, Sèvres porcelain, tapestries, silks, and, of course, pictures.

Her mother however had not complained about the expense of the pictures.

"They are a joy forever!" she said to Salrina. "I am glad that so many by the great European Masters should now belong to this country."

Then as they reached the Chinese Room Salrina could think of nothing but that, incredible though it seemed, she was actually going to meet the heir to the throne, the much-admired but also much-criticised Prince Regent.

He was, as the Earl had warned her, looking portly and no tight-lacing could reduce the size of his stomach.

At the same time he was still extremely good-looking and, although he found it easy to make enemies, he had not lost the art which he had developed as a young man, of making friends, not only with women but also with men of his own age and older.

When the Earl presented Salrina and the Regent smiled at her, she thought his charm radiated out from him and as she curtsied gracefully he said:

"Thank you, Alaric, for bringing me such a lovely guest. You did not exaggerate her attractions."

Salrina felt shy, not only at the compliment the Prince had paid her, but also because it implied that the Earl had praised her.

Then she remembered he would have done so only because he had wanted to get her accepted at Carlton House for a very different reason than her personal looks.

The Chinese Drawing Room seemed already almost filled when they entered it and more people arrived after them, making the numbers for a very large dinner party in the Dining Room.

To Salrina's relief Lord Charles escorted her into dinner and he was seated on her left.

On her right was a garrulous old Member of Parliament who wished to talk only about himself.

She therefore had a chance to look round and admire the highly polished table with its exquisite silver and gold ornaments and the Sèvres porcelain which she was aware had come from France after the Revolution when the Prince had sent his Chef, because he spoke French, to buy furniture from the Palace of Versailles and anything else that he thought his master would appreciate.

Everybody had been astonished at such extravagance at the time on the part of the young Prince.

But Salrina thought now that the exquisite furniture she had noticed on her way to the Dining Room and the pictures that hung on the walls could only increase in value as the years went by, and the Prince's good taste would eventually be appreciated.

Lord Charles, she knew, was as apprehensive as she was of what might happen later, and it was difficult for either of them to think of anything else.

The Earl had already discovered, when he visited Carlton House that morning, who was on the guest list for dinner and he had told Lord Charles and Salrina that they could enjoy the large, rich meal before they started their duties in defending the Prince.

The Earl had given them orders rather, Salrina thought, as if he were addressing his troops before a battle.

"The Frenchman will arrive after dinner," he said,

"when as usual the Prince has invited an enormous number of people to enjoy the garden, if the weather is fine enough, or perhaps the Gothic Conservatory."

He paused for a moment and smiled as he said:

"Salrina will find it is designed like a small Cathedral and quite dazzling in its magnificence!"

He spoke with that dry note in his voice that always puzzled Salrina because she was not quite certain if he was amused or being sarcastic.

"We can only be thankful," Lord Charles said, "that tonight is not one of those fetes which 'Prinny' enjoys when we are deafened by four Bands playing triumphant airs, and the garden is cluttered with huge marquees."

The Earl glanced through the carriage window before he said:

"Since the Regent hates the cold, I guess that tonight, as it is slightly damp, we shall be indoors, which will make it easier for us to keep an eye on him."

When the dinner was over and there were so many *entrées* that Salrina was obliged to refuse one after another, the ladies moved back into the Chinese Room.

When the gentlemen joined them, and other guests began to arrive, it was obvious the Music Room would also be filled with people as would several other rooms opening out of it.

On the Earl's instructions Salrina kept near to the Regent, who had taken up his position in the middle of the room, where he greeted his guests with the same charming affability he had extended to her.

Looking at the women guests who fawned on him and whom she could hear paying him extravagant compliments, Salrina was extremely grateful for Lady Caroline's pretty gown.

It would have been impossible for her to come to Carlton House wearing anything she owned herself.

And how could she possibly have afforded to buy a gown which would have passed muster amongst the women glittering with tiaras, necklaces, bracelets, and corsages of every known precious stone?

Salrina knew that the simple but valuable necklace of pearls which the Earl had lent her was exactly right for a young girl and she thought it showed how knowledgeable he was of women.

Then she looked across the room to see him laughing at something a very beautiful lady, festooned with rubies, was saying to him.

Her décolletage was so low that Salrina blushed when she looked at it.

She thought the Earl looked more amused than she had ever seen him before, and she found herself thinking how dull he must find her beside such sparkling creatures, who were like goddesses.

Then she laughed at her own fancy and thought that everything she was watching was unreal and she had in fact stepped into a theatrical performance without really knowing her part.

Then a very much more frightening thought came into her mind.

Supposing the Frenchman did not appear and there was no attempt of any sort on the Prince's life?

The Earl would then be certain he had been right in his suspicion in the first place that her story was just a trumped-up trick to get herself into what he called the "Holy of Holies."

Because the idea agitated her, Salrina clasped her fingers together until her knuckles showed white.

Mrs. Freeman had not, as she had expected, given her long white kid gloves to wear, but instead had found an exquisite pair of lace mittens which were far more comfortable in the evening and far lighter and more attractive with her gauze and silver gown.

"These were what Lady Caroline always used to wear when she was young," she told Salrina, "and very pretty they always looked. Now she says she's too old, but I thinks she's mistaken!"

Salrina must have shown what she was feeling not only by clasping her hands but by the expression on her face, for she heard Lord Charles say quietly:

"Do not look so frightened, Miss Milton. Somebody might notice it and think you were crossed in love!"

The way he spoke made Salrina laugh, which of course was what he had intended.

She lifted her face up to his and because he was so tall the long line of her neck was very lovely.

Without looking towards him, as if she felt him watching her across the length of the room, Salrina was aware of the Earl.

She thought perhaps he was rebuking her for her inattention, and she knew that while listening to what the lady with the rubies was saying, his eyes were on the Prince and those coming across the room to greet him.

Then because there was so much chatter that it was difficult to hear the names being announced by the Major-domo from the doorway, she only just heard the words: *Saint Cloud*, and realised, although they were said in a very English manner, that it was French.

She tried to see who had arrived, but at that moment the Regent moved from the centre of the room to show the man to whom he had been talking a picture he had recently acquired.

It was hung on the wall just beside the opening into the room which contained his famous miniatures.

A lot of people seemed to have moved with him and as Salrina craned her neck amongst the gentlemen in gold-braided Diplomatic evening dress and soldiers resplendent in uniforms, she suddenly saw only a few feet away from the Prince the top of the head of a smaller man whose face she could not discern.

Quickly, without alerting Lord Charles, she moved past two elegant ladies discussing the latest fashion in bonnets and pushed her way through two gentlemen arguing about the political situation.

At last she saw that standing just in front of the Prince, who was turning from the contemplation of the picture to greet him, was the Frenchman.

It was impossible not to recognise his long nose, his foxy face and dark hair and eyes.

He was dressed in the very height of fashion, except, being a Frenchman, he looked somewhat out of place amongst the less flamboyant Englishmen.

He was holding in his hand a small parcel which she knew was the gift he intended to present to the Prince.

Instantly, as the Earl had told her to do, she dropped the lace handkerchief she held in her hand.

Then, afraid it was obscured by the crowd, she moved nearer to the Prince.

She thought that if the Earl and Lord Charles were caught off their guard, she must somehow warn them in a different manner from what they had arranged.

Then as the Prince gave a welcoming smile to the

newcomer, the assailant held forward the gift he had in his left hand and began to explain in French that he had brought it on behalf of his uncle, the Marquis de St. Cloud.

In the same instant Salrina saw his right hand slip inside his evening coat.

Because she knew what he was about to do, she gave a little scream.

Even as she did so she saw the Earl pushing his way past some beautiful ladies standing beside the Prince, but he was too late.

The Frenchman hearing Salrina's cry looked round and with a swiftness that took her entirely by surprise, he dropped the present he held in his left hand.

Putting his arm roughly around her neck, he dragged her, in the passing of a second, close against him with his back against the wall.

Then he drew with his right hand a long, thin dagger with a sharp point from his coat and held it against her breast.

For a moment there was silence of utter astonishment.

Then he said in French:

"One move and this woman dies!"

Because he was taller than she was, Salrina's head was tipped back and she was vividly aware that she could feel the point of his dagger against her breast through the thin gauze of her gown.

Then, as nobody moved, the Frenchman inched his way along the wall against which he was standing into the open doorway of the Miniatures Room.

Vaguely, because it was difficult to breathe, Salrina saw as if in a haze the Regent's shocked expression and the ladies around him raising their hands to their lips or to their breasts in horror.

Frantically in terror she wanted to look for the Earl, but after one quick glance the Frenchman's movements seemed to make everything swim before her eyes.

She was only aware of the sharp point of the dagger.

She was certain that before he set her free she would die.

When slowly he had edged his way until they were out of the Drawing Room, Salrina, as if somebody were telling her what to do, made an unexpected movement.

As the Frenchman took what was almost the last step backwards through the open doorway, she twisted her right leg round his leg and he stumbled.

It was only a small movement, but as he did so the Earl sprang.

He flung himself almost as if he flew through the air at the Frenchman, knocked his right hand holding the dagger up in the air, and at the same time punched him with all his strength in the face.

Salrina, now free, collapsed onto the carpet and as she did so the Earl punched the Frenchman again on the point of his chin and he slithered slowly down against the wall and fell at his feet.

Then, as pandemonium broke out, Lord Charles picked Salrina up while two *Aides-de-Camp* carried the unconscious Frenchman into the Miniatures Room and out of sight.

As Lord Charles held her, Salrina fought against the faintness that seemed to overwhelm her and the Earl pulled the lapels of his coat back into place.

He did not answer the questions that were being fired

at him from every direction until the Regent, who was always quick to size up a situation, enquired:

"You knew this might happen to me?"

"I was warned, Sir, that it might occur."

"And yet you did not inform me?"

"I thought it might upset Your Royal Highness, and we were prepared and ready to defend you, although I did not expect him to take a hostage."

"I realised it was Miss Milton's action that gave you your opportunity to knock him out," the Regent said with relish. "I must thank her."

Although she was feeling shocked, Salrina managed to curtsy and accepted shyly the Regent's most sincere expressions of gratitude.

"And now, if you will excuse us, Sir," the Earl said, "I think I should take the heroine of the hour home, and hope there will be no more unpleasant incidents to spoil your party."

"I shall not forget this, Alaric," the Regent said, putting his hand affectionately on the Earl's shoulder. "We will talk about it tomorrow."

He thanked Salrina again, and it was with a sense of relief that accompanied by the Earl on one side of her and Lord Charles on the other, they went downstairs to the ball.

They were aware as they left the room behind them that the voices of the guests rose higher and higher.

Only as the Earl placed her in his carriage which came to the front door surprisingly quickly did Lord Charles say:

"If you do not mind, Alaric, I think I will go back for a while. I want to make quite certain that the Frenchman is safely locked up for the night, and I am also rather curious to hear what everybody is saying about you and Miss Milton."

"I can guess that very accurately without listening to it!" the Earl replied sarcastically.

He then climbed into the carriage beside Salrina and Lord Charles went back into the hall.

Salrina was silent not because she had nothing to say, but because she still felt as if she had been caught in a maelstrom and was not certain if her feet were still on the ground.

The Earl understood. He took her hand in his and said:

"It is all over and you were splendid! And it was my fault that because the Prince Regent moved you might have been killed."

"I was afraid you . . . would not see me . . . drop my handkerchief," Salrina faltered.

"I suppose I should have anticipated that might happen," the Earl said angrily.

"You must not blame yourself," Salrina replied, "and your quickness was magnificent, when I had made him stumble, in knocking up his arm before he could . . . kill me."

There was an unmistakable tremor in her voice and the Earl said:

"Forget it. You have been in danger and you have survived. The only thing that matters now is to put it behind you and remember that 'lightning never strikes in the same place twice!'"

Salrina gave a croaking little laugh before she said anxiously:

"Suppose Napoleon tries again with . . . another . . . assailant."

"I doubt it," the Earl replied. "The French do not like

failures, and unsuccessful tactics are never repeated."

It was only a short distance from Carlton House to Berkeley Square and when they arrived the Earl said as they stepped into the hall:

"Would you like a glass of champagne?"

Salrina shook her head.

"I would... like to go to bed... if you do not... mind."

"I think that is very sensible."

She went slowly up the stairs, finding it a comfort to hold on to the banisters to help herself.

The maid who looked after her was already in her bedroom and Salrina undressed almost without speaking and got into bed.

When she was alone she did not blow out the candle but sat back against the pillow, thinking over what had occurred and finding it almost impossible to believe that it had really happened.

How was it possible in Carlton House of all places that she, from the depths of the country and of no social consequence whatsoever, had been able to save the Prince Regent and very nearly lose her own life in the effort?

She had seen when she undressed there was a little red mark on her breast where the point of the dagger had rested.

She knew it was only the Earl's incredibly swift action that had prevented the Frenchman from driving the dagger into her body and then making his escape in the commotion which would have followed.

'Tomorrow I must tell the Earl how grateful to him I am,' she thought.

Then as if there were a dagger in her heart she realised

it was all over and that tomorrow she must go home.

It had been a frightening and embarrassing experience, and yet at the same time wildly exciting, which she would never forget.

She knew if she never saw the Earl or Lord Charles again, she would always feel that they had stepped into her life and had become in a strange way part of herself.

Then she gave a deep sigh and looked round the room.

It would not only be the dramatic events of tonight that she would remember, but the elegance and luxury of Fleet, the beauty of the room in which she was now sleeping, and the incredible treasures of Carlton House.

'I shall think about them and dream about them,' she told herself, and felt it had all been like a fantasy.

Then as she told herself she should go to sleep, a door at the other end of her room near the window opened.

She had realised it was there, but had thought it led into a cupboard or perhaps into an adjoining bedroom.

Now, to her astonishment, the door opened to admit the Earl.

He came across the room towards her, and she saw he had undressed and the white frill of his nightshirt was high against his neck above the long dark-red robe that made him seem as if he had stepped out of some heraldic picture.

As he reached the bed and stood looking down at her, she asked shyly:

"Have you . . . come to . . . say good night to me? I–I . . . forgot to . . . lock the door as I promised I would . . . , but . . . I did not know there was . . . another one."

The Earl smiled.

Then he sat down on the side of the bed facing her.

"I know you are tired, Salrina," he said, "but I want to talk to you because I fancy you are already planning to leave tomorrow."

"Of course," Salrina agreed. "I have to go back to Papa, as you know, but . . . I was just thinking how . . . exciting it has all been . . . and I will never forget staying at Fleet and . . . here in this beautiful room."

"And do you think you will also remember me?" the Earl asked.

Salrina smiled, and he saw her dimples before she said a little shyly:

"I . . . I think it would be . . . impossible to . . . forget you."

"Just as I know it would be impossible for me to forget you!" the Earl said.

He spoke in a voice she had not heard before, and as she looked at him questioningly he said:

"I think, Salrina, you are aware that because we have been through such a traumatic experience together, and also because we have so many things we share in common, it would be impossible to lose each other."

"I . . . I do not . . . understand what you are . . . saying to me," Salrina murmured.

"Shall I say it in a different way?" the Earl asked.

He paused as he spoke, and before Salrina realised what was happening, his arms went round her and his lips took possession of hers.

For a moment it was impossible to breathe, impossible to think.

Then as she knew the Earl was kissing her she was suddenly aware it was something she had wanted and longed for even though she had never expressed it even to herself.

As his lips became more possessive, more demanding against the softness and innocence of hers, she knew that he was part of her fantasy and of her dreams, and part too of the beauty she found everywhere.

But it was more than that.

She could feel the Earl's vibrations, of which she had been aware from the very first, linking her to him, and his kisses made her whole body thrill in a way she had never imagined possible.

It was as if little shafts of sunshine were running through her, making her quiver and making her, although she did not understand, respond to him.

She felt as if he were demanding from her something only she could give him, and she wanted as she had never wanted anything in her whole life, to make him happy.

He raised his head for a moment and when, as she looked up at him, her eyes in the candlelight seemed to fill her whole face with the radiance of the stars, he kissed her again.

Now she could feel his heart was beating against hers, and she felt too there was a strange fire on his lips which she did not understand, but which ignited little flames within her body.

They seemed to burn up from her breast into her throat, to touch the fire on his mouth.

He raised his head again, and now, incoherently, because she felt as if he carried her up into the sky, Salrina said:

"I love . . . you! I . . . I did not . . . know until this moment . . . but I . . . love you!"

"As I love you!" the Earl said in a very deep voice. "I did not imagine any woman could be so sweet, so unspoilt, so utterly and completely natural."

He would have kissed her ágain, but because Salrina was frightened of her own feelings she put up her hands as if to protect herself.

He understood and said with a smile:

"My darling, I have so much to teach you about love."

"I . . . I did not know it was . . . like this!"

"Like what?" he asked.

"Like . . . shafts of lightning running through me . . . or perhaps sunshine . . . except that it . . . burns!"

"That is the beginning," the Earl said. "I will make you burn, my beautiful one, until we are both consumed by our love and you will know that nothing else in the world is of any consequence."

"It is . . . rather . . . frightening!" Salrina whispered.

"Are you still frightened of me, as you were when you first came to Fleet?"

"No . . . not like that," she answered. "I think I am more . . . frightened of myself and . . . what you make me . . . feel."

The Earl laughed and it was a very tender sound.

"I adore you!" he said. "No other woman could express herself in the same way as you do, and I promise you we shall be very, very happy together."

"T-together?" Salrina asked.

"That is something we will talk about tomorrow morning," he said. "It is too late now, and I know how tired you must be. What you have been through has, of course, been very exhausting."

He looked down at her before he said in a very different tone:

"I want you—God knows I want you! But I think for

the first time in my life, I am thinking of someone else rather than myself."

Salrina looked puzzled.

"I . . . I do not understand what you are . . . saying."

"I know it is true!" the Earl said as if he were suddenly aware of the fact. "That is another thing that is so unusual and so completely and absolutley captivating about you."

He bent forward and kissed her cheek before he said:

"Go to sleep and tomorrow we will think of a way of explaining to your father why you cannot return home. Then we will decide where you are going to live, so that I can teach you about love."

Salrina wanted to say again that she did not understand, but his lips were on hers and he kissed her until she felt as if the room disappeared.

They were flying in the darkness of the sky up towards a light which drew them like a magnet and which she thought must be a Heaven where they could be together.

Then as once again she was trembling from the little shafts of lightning that seemed to burn with fire, the Earl sat up.

"You go to my head, Salrina!" he said in a strange voice. "Or rather to my heart! Good night, my lovely one. Leave everything to me, and after tomorrow there will be no more problems and no more lonely nights for either of us."

He kissed her hand, and before she could say anything, before she could even tell him again that she loved him, he walked across the room, turning at the door to smile at her.

Then he was gone.

For a moment Salrina could hardly believe what had happened.

As her whole body vibrated and pulsated with the wonder of his kisses, she told herself she was the happiest and luckiest person in the whole world.

He loved her! He had actually said he loved her! The Earl of Fleetwood, the man whom she had heard about ever since her childhood but had never thought she would even see!

"I love him! I love him!" she said aloud.

As she blew out the light and lay down against the pillows she felt in a strange way as if her mother were beside her.

It was then that for the first time she went back in her mind over what had happened and found it again impossible to understand.

'We will be together, and there will be no more lonely nights,' he had said.

He had spoken as if it were something that would come about immediately before they were married.

It was then, as if the Frenchman's dagger slid into her breast, that she felt it was as cold as ice, that it quenched the little flames of fire within her and left her trembling.

Slowly, as if with an incredible effort, like climbing to the top of a mountain, she went back over everything the Earl had said to her.

Now she listened to it without being swept away by the wonder of his lips and the magnetism of his vibrations.

It was an agony worse than any physical pain to know that while he had told her he loved her and wanted her, she had to face the truth that he did not intend she should be his wife!

When she realised what he did mean, Salrina did not cry. She knew she was past tears.

She only felt as if, having touched the gates of Heaven she had been thrown into the darkness of Hell, and the agony of it was indescribable.

"Mama! Mama!" she found herself whispering. "How could this happen to me? What shall I do?"

She knew that her mother would understand her love.

It was the love she had given to her father from the first moment she had seen him, and her father had loved her in the same way.

He had not suggested anything but that they should be man and wife, and together they had undertaken the long, hazardous, exciting journey to Gretna Green.

But the Earl intended nothing of the sort. She believed that what he was offering her was wrong and wicked, and also, although it seemed so beautiful, was ugly and degrading.

And yet for the moment she could still feel his lips holding her captive, his arms round her and his heart beating against hers.

"I love him! Oh, Mama, I love him!" Salrina murmured aloud. "How can I give him up?"

She had an irresistible impulse to jump out of bed, go to his room, which she was sure was near to hers, and tell him that the love he was offering her was not enough.

And yet at the same time she could not leave him.

Then as the hours passed and the candle beside the bed guttered low and gave very little light, she knew that if she saw the Earl again, every nerve in her body would be straining towards him.

Since with every breath she drew she wanted him more

and more, she might agree to what he was suggesting and find it impossible to refuse anything he asked.

With a little cry, Salrina sat up in bed.

"I must go away!" she said beneath her breath.

She went to the window and pulling back the curtains she saw as the stars were fading that it would not be long before it was dawn.

Almost as if her mother were beside her, helping her, she went to the wardrobe and put on the clothes in which she had arrived, her habit, the little white blouse she wore under it, which had been pressed by the maids.

By the time she was dressed the first faint gold of dawn was breaking low in the sky.

She opened the drawer of the dressing table and took out the three hundred guineas she had received for Orion and put it into the pocket of her jacket.

Then as the dawn brought a faint glow into the bedroom she very softly opened the door.

As she did so she realised that the Earl was sleeping only two doors away from her and for a moment she hesitated.

She was leaving him; she would never see him again. It was an agony beyond anything she had ever imagined she could feel.

Almost as if she were speaking to him, she whispered:

"Good bye! I shall love you all my life . . . but I love you too much to do what you are . . . asking of me!"

The tears came into her eyes, but she would not let them fall.

Afraid she might weaken, she walked along the landing to the top of the stairs and started to descend them carefully, one by one, as if they carried her to the guillotine.

chapter seven

As she heard the iron gates of Fleet close behind her, Salrina felt she was being shut out of Paradise.

Everything had gone more smoothly than she had dared to expect.

She had left the house in Berkeley Square, having asked the night footman who had awoken with a start when she reached the hall:

"Can you tell me the nearest way to a Livery Stables?"

He was still half-asleep and, embarrassed at being caught off-guard, he had stammered as he said:

"It's th' White Bear, Miss. Ye'll find it just down th' road in Piccadilly. Shall I get a carriage fer ye?"

"No, thank you, I will walk," Salrina replied.

Apologetically he said:

"I'm sorry I were asleep, Miss. I'll get into trouble if Mr. Bateson hears about it."

Salrina smiled.

"I will not give you away," she promised. "In return will you do something for me?"

"Yes, Miss, o' course, Miss!"

"Then please do not tell anybody that you have seen me or where I have gone unless His Lordship asks you himself. Then you must tell the truth, otherwise do not volunteer information."

There was a pause as if the footman, who was little more than a boy, struggled to understand what she meant. Then he said:

"I won't say nothin', Miss."

"Thank you," Salrina said, "and I promise I will say nothing about you."

She smiled at him again and hurried through Berkeley Square as quickly as she could.

She found her way into Piccadilly and the first person she met who was a road sweeper told her where the Livery Stables were.

It was a large establishment, and although it was still so early in the morning there were ostlers moving about and a man who seemed to be in charge speaking in a sharp voice.

When he realised that Salrina was a customer he was more cordial, but she thought he looked somewhat disparagingly at her shabby habit.

It was this, she was sure, that made him insist on having half the fare to Fleet in advance.

She was, in fact, horrified at how expensive it would be, but there was nothing she could do but pay it out of the precious three hundred guineas that she had sworn she would never touch.

However, once she was on her way she knew she had

done the right thing and what both her mother and her father would have wished.

At the same time, as every mile the horses travelled put a greater distance between her and the Earl, she knew she had left her heart behind and it would never be wholly hers again.

The horses, although the Post Chaise was very light, were much slower than the Earl's superfine, well-bred team, and when they drew up outside the gates of Fleet it was three hours and twenty minutes since they had left London.

It was, however, still early enough for Salrina to be sure nobody in London would yet have missed her and her maid would be merely waiting for her to ring the bell for her breakfast.

As she thought of the delicious tray brought up to her bedside, the silver coffeepot and cream jug, and the cup and plates of Crown Derby, she knew it was one of the beautiful things she had left behind and would never know again.

The gatekeeper hurried to open the iron gates, and then there was the sight of the house in the morning sunshine looking even more enchanting and more magical, Salrina thought, than it had done before.

Because it was a pain to look at it and to know to whom it belonged, she tried to shut her eyes, but even so, she was aware of the pole on which the Earl's standard flew when he was at home.

She thought it was like him, strong and upright against the sky, and to anybody like herself out of reach.

She went straight to the stables and Jupiter nuzzled against her affectionately as if to tell her how much he had missed her.

Having thanked the grooms and given them one of her precious guineas to be divided amongst them, she set off down the drive, knowing that the sooner she disappeared into obscurity the safer she would be.

As she rode home, finding it far easier to travel across country not having to lead another horse, she jumped hedges and travelled as the crow flies. It was not yet noon when she had her first sight of the thatched cottages of the village she had known all her life.

In the centre of them stood the grey stone Norman Church where she had been Christened and where her mother had been laid to rest.

All the more now she knew that however much she suffered she had done the right thing.

It would have been unthinkable to make her father or mother ashamed of her and to abandon the ideals on which she had been brought up.

Nevertheless, to think of the Earl was an agony, and she knew that whatever he might feel for her, she loved him with every breath she drew, with every thought that entered her mind.

She rode into the Manor through the gate which was never closed because the hinges were rusty, and up the narrow drive which was overgrown with weeds, while the grasses on either side was uncut.

Then in front of her she saw the ancient grey stone house which was her home.

'This is where I belong,' she told herself defiantly, almost as if she were speaking to the Earl. 'I could not bear to be ashamed to come back, or that my father should disown me.'

She rode into the stables and Len grinned at her in a way that told her he was delighted to see her.

As she dismounted, a man she recognised as Rosemary's coachman came from the stables.

"'Mornin', Miss," he said. "Oi'll stable ye 'orse for ye."

"Thank you," Salrina said.

After patting Jupiter she took her bundle from the back of his saddle and walked towards the house.

She felt as she entered the untidy hall with its ancient rugs and threadbare carpet that it was a vivid contrast to the grandeur and luxury of both Fleet and the Earl's house in Berkeley Square.

Then she told herself fiercely that that was unimportant compared with the fact that here in the Manor there was not only love, but the pride that made her mother and father refuse to be crushed or even depressed by their poverty.

They had kept on laughing because their love was much more important than anything else.

She wondered if her father was downstairs or in his bedroom.

She thought she heard voices and opened the door of the Sitting Room, which overlooked the garden and which they always used.

The sunshine was flooding in through the windows and for the moment it was hard to focus her eyes.

Then she saw that sitting at the end of the room with her father, who had his foot resting on a stool, near to him and talking earnestly so that their faces were very close together, was Rosemary.

It took them a second or so to realise she was there.

As they turned to look at her, Salrina had the strange feeling that she had intruded on something very intimate.

It was just a passing thought and before she could

really formulate it Rosemary had jumped to her feet to move towards her.

"Dearest Salrina," she exclaimed, "you are back! I am so glad! Your father and I have been very worried about you!"

"Yes, I am back," Salrina said dully, "and everything is all right. We saved His Royal Highness."

She kissed her father, who put his arms around her to say:

"How could you have got involved in anything so horrifying? I could hardly believe what Rosemary told me was true."

"It was true, Papa," Salrina said, "and the Frenchman was about to stab His Royal Highness with a dagger when the Earl prevented it."

Her father's arms tightened. Then he said:

"Well, thank God it is all over and you are home safely. Never again will I allow you to go away on your own and let this sort of thing happen!"

He spoke sternly, but Salrina knew how worried he had been.

She kissed him again and because she had no wish to talk about herself, she said:

"I hope Rosemary has looked after you and prevented you from trying to do too much!"

Her father's eyes twinkled.

"She bullies me almost as much as you do!"

"That is unfair!" Rosemary exclaimed. "But I have carried out Salrina's instructions and tried to make you get well quickly."

"You have been very kind," Lord Milborne said, "and in fact a ministering angel in every possible way."

The manner in which he spoke and the caressing note

in his voice that Salrina had not heard for a long time made her look first at him, then at Rosemary.

The expression in the latter's eyes told her what she thought she should have known already, that Rosemary was in love with her father, and had been when she used to come to the Manor to give her lessons.

Salrina had been too young to be very observant about other people's emotions, but now it flashed through her mind that when her father came into the room Rosemary's eyes had seemed to light up and she was always eager to take him to the stables to see if they could help him in any way.

'If Papa marries Rosemary...' she told herself, then stopped.

Of course the idea was absurd, and she was sure that such a thing had never entered his mind.

And yet she had the unmistakable feeling that they wanted to be alone together.

"I will go to see Nanny," she said, "and tell her I am back. And actually, as I have had no breakfast, I am very hungry."

"Perhaps we could have luncheon early," Rosemary suggested.

Salrina did not answer, but hurried away from the Sitting Room down the passage to the kitchen.

As she expected, Nanny was preparing luncheon and to her astonishment the young footman who had been on the box of Rosemary's carriage was helping her.

"So you're back!" Nanny cried as Salrina appeared. "And about time too! And what have you been up to, I'd like to know? We've all been in a real flutter about you."

"I am quite safe, Nanny, as you see," Salrina said,

kissing her, "but I have had no breakfast and your cooking smells delicious—"

"You'll have to wait for it!" Nanny interrupted. "But you'll find some biscuits in the tin."

Salrina walked to the tin that had always stood on the dresser ever since she had been a child, but in the last years, when they had been so hard up, had always been empty.

Now to her surprise when she lifted the lid she found not only the shortbread biscuits which Nanny made, and which she had always enjoyed, but also macaroons with an almond in the centre of them.

She looked at them with surprise and, as if she knew what Salrina was going to ask, Nanny sent the footman to get her some milk from the dairy.

"What has been happening, Nanny?" Salrina asked.

"Now don't you go making any trouble, Miss Salrina, because you know what His Lordship's like about accepting things that he can't reciprocate! But Mrs. Whitbread says to me when she comes here:

"'I am not going to be an imposition on the household with three extra mouths to feed, so we will pay for our keep and it is just as easy for you to feed His Lordship with what you feed us, and I will see that he eats what is put in front of him.'"

Salrina laughed.

"You make her sound as if she was Papa's governess!"

"All I'm concerned with," Nanny said tartly, "is that we've had some decent food to eat for a change. We've got chickens and young lamb and the Master's already beginning to look a different man!"

Salrina did not say any more. She took two macaroons out of the tin, put the lid back on tightly, and said:

"I am going upstairs, Nanny. If I stay here I shall eat everything before it even reaches the table!"

"Don't you dare touch anything, Miss Salrina!" Nanny said sharply.

But she was smiling, and as Salrina went up the stairs she thought that even Nanny looked younger and brighter because she was having good food for a change.

She went into her bedroom to take off her riding habit and put on one of the old frocks she had worn for years and which were faded with so many washings and were too tight for her.

She forced herself not to think of the gowns she had been able to borrow from the Earl's sister, but went downstairs to find her father was sitting with a glass of wine in his hand, which was something he had not been able to do for a long time.

"You must have a glass of what the doctor has ordered for me," Rosemary said. "As I said to your father, if there is one thing I hate, it is drinking alone."

There was a look in her eyes that told Salrina it was her tactful way of bringing wine into the house without her father's pride being hurt.

She sipped a little of the delicious golden wine, trying not to remember the champagne that the Earl had given her.

She tried too not to remember him sitting at the Dining Room table laughing with Lord Charles with a glass of brandy in his hand.

For the first time in her life, when luncheon was finished she found she virtually had nothing to do.

She learnt that Rosemary's coachman had taken over the stables and was seeing to the horses, and the footman, when he was not helping Nanny, was exercising them.

It therefore meant that if Salrina wanted to ride, it would be for pleasure and not obligatory because it had to be done.

Although they were trying to include her all the time in their conversation, Salrina knew perceptively that her father and Rosemary wanted to be alone.

She therefore went up to her bedroom and sat disconsolately on her bed.

She was aware that if her father did love Rosemary and she loved him, it would be the best possible thing that could happen where he was concerned. But she knew what a great difference it would make to her own life.

Later in the afternoon, when she came in from the garden, she found Rosemary waiting for her in the hall.

She asked her to go with her into the Morning Room, which was rarely used because it made an extra room to clean, saying:

"There is something I want to tell you, Salrina."

She looked worried, then as Salrina did not speak she said:

"I am afraid you will be upset."

"If you are going to tell me that you love Papa and he loves you, I will not be upset but very, very glad!"

"Do you mean that? Do you really mean it?" Rosemary cried.

"Of course I mean it!"

Rosemary looked at her as if to make sure she was speaking the truth. Then as the tears ran down her cheeks she said:

"Oh, dearest, I am so happy, I can hardly believe after the long years of misery that the man I have loved all my life really cares for me."

"I always thought you were very fond of Papa."

"I love him, I love him with all my heart," Rosemary said. "I always have. I never imagined a man could be so handsome, so charming, and yet..."

She stopped. Then with an effort she went on.

"... and yet I knew how much he loved your mother and how happy they were. Only in the stories I used to tell myself was there a happy ending for me."

Salrina put her arms around Rosemary, kissed her, and said:

"Now I know you will both be very happy. He has been so miserable without Mama, and everything falling about our heads."

"That is another thing I want to talk to you about."

She drew Salrina to the sofa and holding her hand said:

"Would you be angry and very hurt if I suggest to your father, as I have already done, that we buy a house near Newmarket where he could train race horses?"

This was something Salrina had never expected to hear, and for a moment she only stared at Rosemary, who went on.

"I know he will never love me in the same way that he loved your mother, but for his sake as well as mine I think it would be wise to forget the past and start a new chapter, so to speak, where there are not so many things to revive old memories."

She looked apprehensively at Salrina, who cried:

"Of course, you are right! Papa would love more than anything else in the world to own race horses."

"You would be able to help him," Rosemary said quickly.

Salrina did not speak.

It flashed through her mind that if her father was

starting a new life, it would be best for him if she went away for at least a year so that he and Rosemary could be alone.

She knew how much she resembled her mother and that it would be impossible for her father to see her without thinking of the wife he had lost rather than the wife he now had.

She did not however say this, but merely said:

"What we must do, Rosemary, is to plan your wedding. I expect you want your father to marry you?"

Rosemary blushed.

"That was your father's suggestion, but I am not certain I want the whole village staring at me and saying how much I have come up in the world!"

Salrina laughed.

"It will give them something to talk about, and they will enjoy every moment of it. But there is no reason why you should have them staring at you as you marry Papa. You can be married by yourselves very early in the morning. I know that is what I would like to do."

"So would I!" Rosemary agreed. "Oh, Salrina, dearest, I love you, I always have, and you are so kind to me."

She was crying again and Salrina said:

"If you keep crying, Papa will think I am being unkind to you and be very angry with me."

Rosemary laughed through her tears, and Salrina went from the room to tell her father how delighted she was that he had found somebody to look after him.

Rosemary did not accompany her and Salrina said:

"I have worried so much about you, Papa, and I know Rosemary is the right wife for you. She was always the kindest person I have ever known, and as she is very intelligent, I know you will have so many interests in common."

Her father's fingers tightened on her hand as he said:

"You know as well as I do, Salrina, that no one could ever take your mother's place, but I am still a comparatively young man and without her I am very lonely."

"Of course you are, Papa, and the best thing you could possibly have would be a son who could ride your horses when you have become too fat to do so!"

Her father laughed, as she meant him to do.

At the same time she knew from the expression in his eyes that he had already thought of that.

With a little pang in her heart she knew that however much he loved her it was not the same as having a son to inherit his title and, as she had said, race his horses, which as she as a girl was unable to do.

They ate a very lighthearted, happy dinner.

Salrina noticed that her father did not seem to be aware of how much the food had improved.

He accepted the quite elaborate menu, and also the champagne which appeared as if by magic, and Rosemary said they must drink each other's health.

Afterwards, when Salrina had come up to bed, she could hear them laughing downstairs for a long time before she knew her father was being helped up the stairs by the footman who also had constituted himself his valet.

'There is nothing left for me to do,' she thought.

Then because she could not stop herself she cried helplessly for the Earl before she finally fell asleep.

*   *   *

The next two days were spent making plans for Salrina's father and Rosemary to visit Newmarket in search of a house with the sort of stabling they would require.

Because Lord Milborne's leg was now much better and the Doctor had said if he was careful he could use it sparingly, he could move freely about the house and visit the horses.

It was Rosemary who decided they should leave on Friday to stay with some friends who lived outside Newmarket, and who had replied when she had sent a letter by post chaise that they were delighted to have them as their guests.

"He is an elderly man who knew my husband," Rosemary said to Salrina, "and he is very knowledgeable, and will, I know, find us exactly the sort of house and stabling that your father is looking for."

Then almost as if it were an afterthought she added:

"I know you will enjoy meeting him."

Salrina shook her head.

"It is sweet of you, dearest, but I am not coming with you."

"Why not?"

"For two reasons," Salrina replied, "the first, because I think you and Papa should be alone, the second because until I can buy myself some new clothes I really would look like the beggarmaid at the feast!"

Rosemary gave a little cry.

"Oh, dearest, I had not forgotten you needed clothes, and I was planning we should go together, as soon as possible, to buy in the vicinity what you need, and then when we return from Newmarket, to take you to London and buy you the loveliest gowns any débutante has ever had!"

Salrina did not protest; she merely kissed Rosemary and said:

"That is just the sort of thing you would think of, but I am quite content to wait here with the horses until you come back. First things first, and when you have sorted out Papa you can then turn your attention to me!"

Rosemary laughed.

"You are making me sound like a bossy woman!"

"I think really you are, as Papa said, an angel sent down from Heaven especially to help us."

Rosemary hugged her as she said:

"That is what I want to be. Oh, Salrina, is it not wonderful, marvellous, and exciting that I am rich enough to do all the things I have wanted to do for the people I love!"

A day later, after they were married and her father set off for Newmarket, there were three new employees in the stables for Salrina to supervise in looking after the horses.

Nanny also had three girls from the village to clean the house under her instructions.

Salrina waved them good-bye, then went back into the house knowing that her father seemed younger and better-looking than he had for years.

She knew that Rosemary was already planning to take him first to the best tailors in Newmarket, then as soon as they reached London to Savile Row.

Strangely enough, because her father now by law had the handling of all Rosemary's money, he did not seem to resent that she had paid his debts and that it was through her that he was, to all intents and purposes, a rich man.

Salrina knew it was Rosemary's exquisite tact and

diplomacy that had made everything so easy.

Salrina had been tactful too because when they were married very early the previous morning, she had not been a witness at the ceremony.

Instead she had stayed at home and with Nanny had prepared the table for the Wedding Breakfast with every white flower she could find in the garden.

She had polished the ancient silver *entrée* dishes which had seldom been removed from the safe since her mother's death, until they shone like mirrors.

"I never thought happiness would be back in this house like sunshine!" Nanny said as they waited for the newly-wed couple to come from the Church.

"Papa is very, very lucky to have Rosemary," Salrina replied.

At the same time she knew that if she was honest, the feeling that had never left her heart was all the more agonising today than it had ever been.

She felt lonely and the house seemed very quiet and empty when Rosemary and her father had driven away down the drive.

She felt sure they would be holding hands and Rosemary would be telling him not only in words but by the look in her eyes how much she adored him.

"It is something I will never be able to say to any man," Salrina sighed.

She went into the Sitting Room to look at the portrait of her mother that hung on one wall.

"What am I to do with myself, Mama?" she asked, feeling that if she listened she might hear her mother answer her question.

The door opened and because there were tears in her eyes, and she thought Nanny might see them, she turned hastily away from the picture to walk towards the mantelpiece.

Then when Nanny did not speak she turned to see what she wanted, and was suddenly very still.

It was not Nanny who had come into the room as she had thought, but the Earl.

For a moment, because he was always so vividly in her thoughts, she felt she must be imagining him, that he had materialised out of her mind and had no substance in fact.

Then as he moved slowly towards her she knew he was real and felt her heart start to beat violently within her breast, and it was difficult to breathe.

She had an irresistible impulse to run towards him, fling herself against him, and ask him to kiss her just once before she sent him away as she knew she had to.

Then as if her mother were watching her from her portrait and she knew that she must behave as a lady, she lifted her chin a little, afraid he would hear the thumping of her heart.

He came nearer and still nearer until he stood facing her. Then he said:

"I have come to tell you how sorry I am for the way I behaved."

It was not what Salrina had expected him to say, and she could only stare at him, her eyes so wide they seemed to fill her whole face.

He was looking at her as if he had never seen her before, and as if he would imprint her face on his consciousness so that he would never forget it.

Then with a slight twist of his lips he said wryly:

"I am apologising for the third time. It is becoming a habit! All the same, how could you have done anything

165

so utterly damnable as to slip away without telling me you were leaving?"

There was silence before Salrina said:

"I . . . I had to . . . go!"

"Why?"

She felt the color come into her cheeks and her eyes flickered before she said in a voice that was almost a whisper:

"I could not . . . do what you . . . wanted."

"Of course not! It was crazy of me, wicked of me, even to suggest it! But you have bewildered and bemused me ever since I have known you, and love made it impossible for me to think clearly."

She did not quite understand what he was saying and after a moment she asked:

"H-how did you . . . find me?"

"Quite by chance, after you had nearly driven me mad!" the Earl replied. "How could you be so unfeeling, so inhuman, as to make me suffer in a way no woman has ever made me suffer before?"

"I think you are . . . joking."

"I am telling you the truth!" the Earl said sharply. "Yet when I was desperate, I might have known that fate, luck, or perhaps God would be on my side."

"What . . . happened?"

"I had been to see your friend Mabel, who lied very unconvincingly, but I could not force the truth out of her."

"You knew she was . . . lying?"

The Earl smiled for the first time.

"Of course I knew she was lying. I am not entirely insensitive!"

"I . . . know that."

"Just as I can read your thoughts and know your feelings," he went on, "so I am usually aware when people do not tell me the truth that they are hiding something important."

"I am not . . . important!"

"You are to me!"

She looked away from him again, thinking if he pleaded with her she would find it impossible to resist him. Yet she must fight him by every means that she could.

"I left Honeysuckle Cottage, or whatever it is called," the Earl said, "then as I did so one of my neighbours who was passing by in his Phaeton bade me good day."

"'I expected to see you at the Steeplechase, Fleetwood,' he said. 'In fact, I would have backed you as the winner.'

"'I had other things to do,' I replied.

"'I hope she was pretty!' My friend laughed. 'I wish you had seen the consternation there was when young Carstairs, who has always been a cocky young fellow, won it!'

"I vaguely remembered," the Earl went on, "that Carstairs farmed a considerable amount of Sir Robert Abbot's land, and I said to my friend:

"'It must have been a very poor entry this year for a local man to win the Steeplechase!'

"'He had a good horse.'

"I suppose I looked surprised, for my friend went on.

"'An exceptional horse, as it happens! Best jumper I have seen for years! I wish I had bought him myself!'

"'Where did Carstairs get a horse like that?' I enquired.

"'From Milborne, who of course trained him. I shall certainly visit him in the next day or two and see if he

167

has anything in the same category.'

"'Milborne?'" I repeated, the Earl continued. "'I seem to know the name.'

"'Of course you do,' my friend said. 'Your father was very fond of Lord Milborne and his very pretty wife—one of the nicest couples in the County, except that they are as poor as Churchmice!'

"'Then I must certainly call on them one day,' I said, 'and make myself pleasant, but at the moment I am rather busy.'

"'Not "them,"' my friend corrected. 'Lady Milborne is dead, but actually they have a very pretty daughter who is an exceptional rider.'"

The Earl paused. Then he said:

"It was then as if I were being prompted that I asked:

"'A pretty daughter? What is her name?'

"'Now, let me think,' my friend replied. 'It is rather unusual—Salrina—yes, that is right—Salrina!'"

"So . . . that was how you . . . found me!" Salrina murmured.

"That conversation took place yesterday evening," the Earl said, "after I had searched the whole of London because I could not believe you would go home without waiting to hear what had happened to our prisoner, and of course receiving the grateful thanks of His Royal Highness for saving his life."

"It was you who did that," Salrina corrected, "when you knocked the Frenchman down."

"It was *you* who knew about the plot, *you* who took us to Carlton House, and *you* who were clever enough to trip him and give me the opportunity of knocking him out."

The Earl smiled at her and he added:

"The Prince Regent is very glad to be alive, and he had invited you not only to a Reception where he can thank you formally, but also to another of his evening parties which will be even more boring than the one the other night!"

"How could you say it was boring?" Salrina protested.

Then once again she realised that the Earl was teasing her as he remarked:

"I thought we might go together."

Because she knew she must refuse and thought it might make him angry, she said:

"You have not told me what . . . happened to the . . . Frenchman."

It suddenly struck her that if there was a trial she might have to give evidence and suddenly she felt very frightened.

"The best thing that could possibly have happened to him," the Earl replied.

"What was that?"

"Although the *Aides-de-Camp* took away the dagger with which he had threatened you, he had another in the lining of his coat. On the way to the Tower, he stabbed himself through the heart. He is dead!"

Salrina drew in her breath. It was sigh of relief.

"You might also be interested to know," the Earl went on, "that it was the Regent who identified the Englishman."

"I had forgotten about him!"

"He is a disreputable character who tried to cheat His Royal Highness by selling him a fake picture which he swore on the Bible was genuine. The Regent turned him out of Carlton House and had him blackballed from all his Clubs."

Salrina knew what a punishment this would be to an Englishman and listened intently as the Earl continued.

"He therefore swore to have his revenge and must have been in communication with the French, which was not difficult because he had been smuggling in quite a large way for over a year."

"What will happen to him?"

"He will be shot as a traitor to his country," the Earl said harshly.

Salrina did not speak and after a moment very quietly he said:

"That accounts for everybody except you and me, Salrina."

Salrina clasped her hands together before she answered:

"I . . . I am sorry I put you to . . . so much trouble . . . but I went away because I . . . could not . . . do what you . . . suggested."

"I have already apologised for that, and I really have no excuse, except that I did not expect my future wife to ride about the country without a groom, or to be so adventurous, so sweet, unspoilt, and utterly adorable that I was not thinking clearly!"

As he spoke Salrina's eyes were on his and she felt as if he hypnotised her with every word.

Then as she asked beneath her breath:

"D-did you . . . say your . . . future wife?"

The Earl moved towards her.

Very slowly he put his arms around her and drew her against him.

"I love you, Salrina, and actually it does not matter at all what your name is. I want you because I feel incomplete and lost without you. You are everything I have been looking for all my life."

The last words were spoken close against her mouth, then his lips were on hers.

He pulled her closer and still closer to him, and to Salrina it was as if the Heavens opened and he carried her into the glory of the sun, and there was the singing of angels.

Because she had been so unhappy, because she had missed him so terribly, she felt now as if he were making her a part of him and she was no longer alone.

She was so completely his that even a wedding ceremony could not make them any closer.

"I love you! I love you!" she wanted to say.

But the Earl was kissing her fiercely, demandingly, passionately, as if he thought he had lost her and was making sure she could never escape him again.

He kissed her until they were both breathless, then he raised his head and said:

"How can you be so utterly, completely different from anyone else I have ever known? How can you make me feel as I thought it impossible to feel for any woman?"

"How do you . . . feel?" Salrina whispered.

"Wildly, ecstatically happy!" he replied. "But still desperately afraid that I might lose you again."

His arms tightened until he hurt her as he said:

"As that is something I intend to prevent, we are going to be married at once. I have no intention of gambling on what I know is my whole future happiness."

Salrina made a little murmur and hid her face against his neck.

"Can I . . . really marry . . . you?"

"You are going to marry me!" the Earl said firmly.

"Ever since I have known you you have been unpredictable, and when you disappeared I could only curse myself for my stupidity and be more afraid than I have ever been of any enemy, gun, or cannon!"

Salrina laughed.

"I am sure that is not true!"

"I will make you believe me by making sure that you are my wife, and keeping you with me by day and by night!"

He gave a little groan as he said:

"The only unselfish thing I have ever done, when I was wanting you so overwhelmingly, was to leave you the other night when you were tired. It was like sticking a thousand daggers into my body to go back to my empty bed alone!"

Salrina thought of what an agony it had been for her to leave him the next morning, but she merely made a little murmur against his neck, and she knew he kissed her hair before he went on.

"I believe, my darling, that we are going to be very happy in the future. We have so many things in common, even though we need not spend all our time looking for French spies and saving the Regent's life!"

It was then that Salrina raised her head to look at him with a worried expression in her eyes.

"Please . . . listen to me," she pleaded.

"I would rather kiss you!"

"No . . . please . . ."

"What do you want to say?"

"Only that I . . . do not think you ought to . . . marry me," she said hesitatingly. "You see . . . I have never . . . lived in your world . . . and I know nothing about it . . . or the people who are . . . important to . . . you."

She made a little sound that was like a sob before she went on.

"I shall make . . . mistakes and perhaps you will be ashamed . . . of me . . . or else become . . . bored . . . and that would be even . . . worse than . . . losing you now."

"I shall not be bored and you will not lose me," the Earl said firmly. "I cannot think why you should feel you would be upset or embarrassed by my friends, or the Prince Regent for that matter."

Salrina laughed, but there was a touch of fear in it.

"You . . . do not understand. This is where I have lived all . . . my life. Look around you and you will see how very poor we have been. So poor that we have often been hungry. I have never been to parties or met smart people, and I never had a decent gown to wear until you lent me . . . one of your sister's."

She thought as she spoke that she was throwing away something so infinitely precious that she would regret it all her life.

At the same time, because she loved him, she had to be honest, and she loved him enough to want his happiness even more than her own.

As if he understood, the Earl said in a different tone from what he had used before, and which was quiet and tender:

"It is because your life has been different, my darling, that you are so different. Do you not understand it will be very exciting and very thrilling for me not only to give you all the things you have missed, but to look after you, help you not to make mistakes, and to know that unlike the other women there have been in my life you will be mine—completely and absolutely mine!"

His arms tightened, then he said:

"More than anything else, I want to teach you, my beautiful, about love. I adore your ignorance, your shyness, and the way you are completely unspoilt."

He drew in his breath before he said:

"I could no more be bored with you than if I were touching one of the stars, which is something we will do together."

Salrina remembered how her mother had said:

"A woman must always help her husband to aim for the stars, even though they seem out of reach."

"Will you let me do things with you?" she asked. "You are so clever, so brilliant. I know there are so many people you can help, and there will be so much to do for England when the war is over. You can lead, guide, and inspire the people who will follow you."

She saw the surprise in the Earl's eyes as she added:

"Please . . . let me be with you and help . . . if only in a . . . tiny way."

"I know from what you have said it will not be a 'tiny' way, but a very large way," the Earl replied, "and, Salrina, you are so perfect that I can hardly believe I have been fortunate enough to find you."

He looked at her for a long moment before he said:

"You have not answered my question—how soon will you marry me? For I do not intend to wait one second longer than is necessary."

Salrina laughed and it was a sound very near to tears as she answered:

"Now! This moment! If I can be your wife, I swear I will try to make you happy and will love and worship you forever!"

Then the Earl's lips found hers and he kissed her at

174

first almost reverently as if she were something very precious and sacred.

Then as she knew she excited him she felt the fire burning once again on his lips and flickering flames rise within herself.

It was so glorious, so perfect, and at the same time so much part of the Heaven she thought she would never find again, that she surrendered herself completely to his kisses, feeling his heart beating frantically against hers.

After a long time he raised his head to ask in a curiously unsteady voice:

"Now what do you feel?"

"That I am in Paradise!"

As she spoke Salrina remembered how when she left Fleet she thought she was being shut out of Paradise.

"And you are happy?"

"Wonderfully . . . gloriously . . . marvellously happy and very . . . very . . . e-excited."

At the last word Salrina stammered and shyly hid her face.

The Earl however put his fingers under her chin so that he could look at her.

"Does that still frighten you?" he asked.

"Not really," she whispered. "But perhaps you will be shocked if my love makes me very . . . wild and . . . unrestrained."

The Earl laughed, and it was a very tender sound, before he said:

"My sweet, my darling . . . could anyone be more alluring? I adore you."

"You will not . . . be shocked?"

"I am only afraid of my shocking you. But I think,

my precious, the fires of love will burn for both of us."

Then he kissed her until she was no longer on earth but moving in the sky among the stars to a Paradise that was made for them by God.

The Earl knew they had both found the perfection of love that all men seek, but only a few are privileged enough to attain.

"I love you! God, how I love you!" he said hoarsely.

Then he was kissing her again and Salrina knew there was no need for words.

It was love which was in her heart, in her mind, in her soul, and in her body.

Love, that made her belong to him and him to her, and there was no escape for either of them.

Songs with the Royal Philharmonic Orchestra.

In 1976 by writing twenty-one books, she broke the world record and has continued for the following seven years with twenty-four, twenty, twenty-three, twenty-four, twenty-four, twenty-five, and twenty-three. She is in the *Guinness Book of Records* as the best-selling author in the world.

She is unique in that she was one and two in the Dalton List of Best Sellers, and one week had four books in the top twenty.

In private life Barbara Cartland, who is a Dame of the Order of St. John of Jerusalem, Chairman of the St. John Council in Hertfordshire and Deputy President of the St. John Ambulance Brigade, has also fought for better conditions and salaries for Midwives and Nurses.

Barbara Cartland is deeply interested in Vitamin Therapy and is President of the British National Association for Health. Her book *The Magic of Honey* has sold throughout the world and is translated into many languages. Her designs "Decorating with Love" are being sold all over the U.S.A., and the National Home Fashions League named her in 1981, "Woman of Achievement."

Barbara Cartland's Romances (a book of cartoons) has recently been published in Great Britain and the U.S.A., as well as a cookery book, *The Romance of Food*, and *Getting Older, Growing Younger*.

More romance from
BARBARA CARTLAND

Called after her own
beloved Camfield Place,
each Camfield novel of love
by Barbara Cartland
is a thrilling, never-before published
love story by the greatest romance
writer of all time.

October '85...LOVE IS A GAMBLE
November '85...A VICTORY FOR LOVE